THE GUEST
CHILDREN

THE GUEST CHILDREN

A NOVEL

Patrick Tarr

NEW YORK

Books should be disposed of and recycled according to local requirements. All paper materials used are FSC compliant.

This is a work of fiction. All of the names, characters, organizations, places and events portrayed in this novel are either products of the author's imagination or are used fictitiously. Any resemblance to real or actual events, locales, or persons, living or dead, is entirely coincidental.

Copyright © 2025 by Patrick Tarr

All rights reserved.

Published in the United States by Crooked Lane Books, an imprint of The Quick Brown Fox & Company LLC.

Crooked Lane Books and its logo are trademarks of The Quick Brown Fox & Company LLC.

Library of Congress Catalog-in-Publication data available upon request.

ISBN (hardcover): 979-8-89242-298-7
ISBN (paperback): 979-8-89242-312-0
ISBN (ebook): 979-8-89242-299-4

Cover design by Jocelyn Martinez

Printed in the United States.

www.crookedlanebooks.com

Crooked Lane Books
34 West 27th St., 10th Floor
New York, NY 10001]

First Edition: August 2025

The authorized representative in the EU for product safety and compliance is eucomply OÜPärnu mnt 139b-14, 11317 Tallinn, Estonia, hello@eucompliancepartner.com, +33757690241

10 9 8 7 6 5 4 3 2 1

For B and B

PART 1

FRANCES AND MICHAEL

CHAPTER 1

After the bomb killed their mum and dad, Frances dragged Michael from the ruin of their home and ran into the smoke-shrouded street looking for help. Air-raid sirens wailed across the city as the ack-acks fired on Luftwaffe planes and spotlights stabbed the darkness overhead. A barrage balloon, halfway free of its moorings, slumped across the guttering orange skyline.

Frances knew she mustn't panic, although she could see fires blazing in three other buildings close by. It was possible that all of London would burn and crumble on this night, her city reduced to humps of toppled stone and charred wood. She was frightened, so Frances told herself that her mum and dad would be all right—even though she'd seen their bodies, and she knew that they wouldn't. Frances lied to herself so she could devote all her attention to minding Michael. At nine, he was her younger brother by only two years, but Michael was a timid, scattered boy—far more childlike than his years could excuse.

Michael carried his stuffed bear, Stanley, dangling from one hand. The bear was already old and ragged, with uneven and mismatched eyes. He was coated with brick dust now too, his feet bouncing across the rubble as Michael walked. Frances thought Michael was far too old for Stanley, but Mum and Dad always refused to tell him so. She supposed it was her job now.

As they passed a raging house fire, her skin prickled in the heat. Still more sirens cried out in the distance. The noise was unlike anything she'd ever heard. Frances feared her own screams would soon add to the din. Looking to the fire before her, she couldn't even recall which building it used to be, but in that moment she was just grateful for its warmth. Michael looked back to her, his brown eyes glittering in the firelight. Stanley's black ones glittered too, and Frances was glad then that they had the old bear along with them.

She heard the strange, tinkling sound of footsteps coming through the brick rubble. A shadow appeared through the smoke. With the flames behind it, the figure drawing close upon them looked like some dark angel, come to harvest dead souls. Frances froze in place, hoping that if she remained still enough, the apparition wouldn't find her there.

Michael was always ill at ease with strangers. Quite unreasonably so, Frances thought. But when her brother saw someone approaching through the ruin of the street, he ran towards them, wailing, with his arms outstretched.

THE GUEST CHILDREN   5

Frances held back, still frozen, until she saw the upturned bowl shape of the National Fire Service helmet on the man's head. When she saw that, Frances dashed to the fireman so quickly that she tripped over a brick and skinned both her knees raw.

She was up and running again before she even felt the sting.

★ ★ ★

Chapter 2

The Hawksby children were passed off from guardian to guardian, each one brimming with a chipper energy and optimism that both confused and irritated Michael.

He knew that everything wasn't going to be all right, no matter what they cooed at him while they squeezed his shoulders through his borrowed shirt. With each new person trying to reassure him, Michael sank further into a certainty that things could only become worse.

The Hawksbys found themselves with a group of children travelling to Paddington station. None of the chaperones would tell them where they were going, only that they had a grand voyage ahead. Michael assumed the secrecy was required because enemy spies were skulking around, eager to snuff out all surviving sons and daughters of the Crown.

Michael tried to speak to some of the other children on the train once or twice, but he always said peculiar things. He knew this because they would scrunch up their faces at him and giggle before long. Whenever that happened,

THE GUEST CHILDREN 7

Frances would notice and yank him away to a corner. He didn't like how Frances acted like she was his mum sometimes, but Michael knew that he was a dawdler. It was best if he just did what Frances said.

They had their suitcases with them for the journey and wore cards tied to their lapels, with numbers and their full names. Someone had gone to salvage some of their things from the house. Other items were provided for them, including woollen jumpers that were far too big.

Before they left for the station, Frances read out to Michael what the suitcases were meant to contain: "One gas mask, one coat, one cardigan, one hat, one pair of gloves, one dress, two pairs of stockings, one change of knickers etc., one pair of shoes, two pairs of pyjamas, one towel, one hairbrush, and a Bible or New Testament."

"I don't wear dresses or stockings."

"This is the girls' one, Michael. I'll do the boys' one next. But as I'm sure you can imagine, it has shirts and trousers and socks instead."

Michael peered at Stanley in his lap. "They'll let me bring him, won't they?"

"I'll tell them they must, Michael. Please, let's not speak of Stanley anymore."

The night after the train arrived, their chaperones took them to a school where they slept on straw mattresses on the floor. After dinner, they heard air-raid sirens and some distant bombs falling. The chaperones led them in cheery songs, but Michael could tell that their minders were frightened. He could hear it in the strained pitch of their singing voices.

He heard someone say they were in Liverpool, bound for Canada. Liverpool was already the farthest he had ever been from home. Tomorrow they would board a ship and he'd be a whole world away. Michael thought about the last thing he heard his father say.

Stay here, my darlings, back in a jiff.

Michael was certain his father had never lied to him before. His sister and everyone else might believe that his mum and dad were dead, but that didn't make it so. He hadn't seen them himself. He only took Frances's word for it. And Frances wasn't right about everything.

One night on the voyage, Michael sought out one of the chaperones to ask her a question. The chaperone he chose was the youngest of them, with bottle-thick eyeglasses and a limp. He thought she'd be the least likely to make fun of him.

"How will they find us?"

She frowned. "How will who find you, love?"

"Our parents. If we're all the way in Canada, I mean. Will they be given our address?"

"Oh . . ." The chaperone's mouth twitched a little, then she stroked his cheek with her thumb and said, "Don't mind that. You've got a sister to keep safe, and that's the thing."

But Michael did mind. Given his father's promise to return, he wasn't going to leave even the slimmest chance ignored. He carried a small leather journal to collect his

THE GUEST CHILDREN

memories of their travels. Between his entries, he'd sometimes tear out pages to write tiny, folded notes.

Michael and Frances Hawksby were here.

He'd leave a note at every stop on their journey. Michael thought the notes could be like Hansel's crumbs, except birds wouldn't eat the paper the way they'd eaten the crumbs in the fairy tale. Frances could act as lordly as she liked on the journey, but Michael would be the one to make sure Mum and Dad found their way back to them.

★ ★ ★

CHAPTER 3

Frances wasn't supposed to know that another ship carrying Guest Children to Canada had been sunk just a few days earlier, but she'd heard people whispering about it on deck. She didn't tell Michael because he was too anxious already, even without this news. The knowledge was her burden to carry, Frances thought, just as Stanley was his.

The chaperones were jolly, and the ship's crewmen made the endless lifeboat drills as entertaining as they could. There were games and songs, as well as studies, and Frances noted that even Michael was getting into the good spirit of the voyage. The meal on their first night aboard, after their spell of rationing in London, felt fit for a princess and prince, with roast beef and potatoes, carrots and peas, and even some tinned pears in syrup.

Everyone was so kind, and much of the time it all felt like a grand adventure. Sometimes, though, when they didn't realize she was looking, Frances saw disquiet in the sailors' eyes. She heard whispers all over the ship of the

THE GUEST CHILDREN   11

great danger of crossing the Atlantic—of the shadowy U-boats stalking their convoy from below. But there were Royal Navy ships along as their escorts, and Frances knew that the men on board would be brave and clever. If the enemy tried to sneak up on them, they'd get an awful surprise.

One night, Frances heard shouting on deck and felt muffled explosions quivering through the ship's steel hull. Donning her life jacket, she snuck out of their berth and made her way along the narrow corridors, slipping up two sets of metal stairs until she was on deck.

Creeping around to a vantage point by the lifeboats, Frances watched a burning ship sinking into the black night sea, the hull yawning open like a jagged length of pipe. She could see lifeboats in the water, and some men in there as well, floating and waving their arms. There was so much noise, she couldn't even hear their shouts. Frances could barely see the other ships manoeuvring around the survivors, just searchlights twirling ghostly circles in the smoky dark.

Frances was startled when she felt someone take her hand. She turned to see her brother standing next to her, his gas mask over his shoulder and the old bear by his side. She was cross that he'd followed, because Michael would not be able to see such things without later inflicting his screaming nightmares upon her in their berth, but Frances badly wanted to remain and see what would happen to the floating men. Against her better judgment, she let him stay.

There was a great hollow boom, and flame blossomed out from the sinking ship, briefly blinding her. She heard Michael shout in distress and realized with horror that he was clambering over the ship's rail. Frantic, Frances grabbed at his legs and pulled him back.

"Stop it, Michael! What are you doing!"

Michael wept and wriggled. "It's Stanley, they got Stanley!"

Frances pulled Michael back down to the deck and scolded him to stay put, but she kept a hand on him to be sure. She could just make out Stanley, floating on his back in the water below. Startled by the blast, Michael had dropped him overboard. She felt bad for the poor old bear, but still had an unkind urge to tell Michael she'd warned him not to drag the thing around everywhere. It served her brother right, but she didn't need to tell him so.

Michael howled and stuck his head through the rail to look down at Stanley in the water. A crewman heard the commotion and came over in a rush, asking what on earth they were doing on deck, as it was no place for children. He tried to pull them away, but Frances still felt an urgent need to see what would happen to the other ships, and to their own.

The crewman took up Michael's grief-rigid body in one strong arm and held out a hand for Frances, but she made him wait before she finally took it. Michael screamed and wept, reverting to the name he used to call his bear when he was still having trouble with his words. "Stambly . . ."

THE GUEST CHILDREN 13

Frances could hear the men in the water shouting now too, calling for help. In that moment, she became convinced that Michael's hysterics would drown them out and make it harder for the rescuers to find them. Thinking herself clever, Frances grabbed the gas mask hanging from Michael's shoulder and roughly pulled it down over his head to muffle his wailing.

Still, her brother screamed and screamed. The lenses of the mask turned milky-white with the fog of his sorrow, as his body dissolved into trembles over the crewman's shoulder.

* * *

Chapter 4

After disembarking in Halifax, the children went through medical exams, then were put on one train west to Toronto and another north towards their aunt and uncle.

It was near dark when their silent chaperone deposited them at the marina on Lake Carver. From there, they were to travel by boat to the place called Glass Point Lodge. The man who met them was gruff and stooped, and he had what Frances thought was a German accent. Her mistrust was intense and immediate. The accent seemed to raise their chaperone's eyebrows as well, but she said nothing.

The marina man had a long grey beard that was stained orangey-yellow in places. After they waited for their things to be loaded into the boat, he put something in his mouth and started to chew. Frances hadn't seen men chew tobacco before and was curious how it worked. Once she saw him spit, she stopped looking.

The chaperone left, and the man growled at them to get into the boat. It was a patchy craft, made of old wood, with

THE GUEST CHILDREN 15

a small motor attached to the back that the man turned to steer. Frances watched in silence as they passed a few small cabins perched by the water. She looked to the wall of high trees surrounding the lake, towering above great swaths of old stone the old man told them was part of the Canadian Shield.

Michael asked if the shield would be strong enough to withstand German bombs. The man went funny and quiet before he said yes, it probably would.

Frances wondered whether a U-boat could find its way to this lake. She imagined one breaching the surface of the water, leaping up in a raging surge of froth, guns levelled at them and a man on a loudspeaker shouting for their surrender. She wanted to ask the marina man, whose name she'd learned was Mr. Schust, if it was possible that a U-boat could reach them there, but she didn't want to seem foolish or to cause offence.

As the boat drew close to a narrow channel out of Lake Carver, Frances saw Mr. Schust's hand tighten on the outboard motor's handle as he slowed down. They passed through the channel, which had a little stone cottage on one side. It was twilight now, quickly turning dark as the sun disappeared behind the trees at the far end of the lake behind them.

When they came out onto a smaller lake, Frances asked, "Is this the same water?"

"Hmm?"

"Why is the water a different colour here?"

16 Patrick Tarr

"Different runoff, different soil under the water. Different lake."

There were no cottages on this little lake. At least, none that Frances could see. It was the last of the twilight now, and she expected she'd see some lights or fires if there were. Faced with the isolation of where they'd be billeted until the war was over, Frances got a suffocating feeling, as if she'd stayed underwater for too long. She wished she could turn to her brother for comfort, but Frances worried that if she showed Michael her dread, it would only make him plummet so much further into his own dark places. That was just how he was.

"Where are all the people?"

"Further spread out here than what you're used to, I should think."

Michael started talking then, perhaps to distract himself. He told Mr. Schust that they were going to live with their mother's sister, Aunt Theresa, and her husband, Uncle Simon.

"We've never met them before. We don't know what they're like, but they own the Glass Point Lodge. Uncle Simon was at the High Commission in Ottawa, then he and Aunt Theresa decided to buy an inn and stay here. My mother said it was a silly idea. They had a boy around my age, but he died. Do you know them?"

"No."

"Did you know Gerald? That was the boy's name."

"No."

Frances thought it strange that Mr. Schust said no more than that. He didn't even remark that poor Gerald's death was a shame. He just turned away from them to study the dark lake ahead as the boat sliced through the water. She watched his hand tighten on the tiller again, noticing now that the back of it was pink and bumpy with scars, like the burned skin of some of the Great War veterans she'd seen in the street.

Michael pointed to some big trees swaying along the shore and asked what was moving in there to make that happen. Mr. Schust said it was just the wind, but Frances wondered how it was that the wind was moving only those trees, and not all the other ones ringing the lakefront.

She could tell Michael was wondering the same thing.

CHAPTER 5

By the time the boat came to Glass Point, which looked like a bony finger jutting off the shore, it was fully dark. Michael had never seen such darkness. In the shrouded moonlight, Michael could just make out the outline of a building as they drew near the dock. At first he thought that was the lodge, but soon he realized it was just a boat-house, and that the larger stone and wood resort loomed behind it. There looked to be a faint yellow glow in one or two of the upper windows, and Michael thought he saw the shape of a person looking out from one. He wondered who it might be.

Frances asked Mr. Schust a question then, but Michael couldn't hear it over the noise of the motor. He imagined that Mr. Schust couldn't either, because he didn't answer, or even react. His whole body looked tight now, like a statue of a boatsman, and he stared straight ahead, seeming to have forgotten the tobacco in his mouth.

As they came up to the dock, Michael saw two shadows

carrying lanterns coming down to meet them. This was his Aunt Theresa and Uncle Simon, Michael had to assume. He was excited to meet them, but afraid they wouldn't be nice and he'd have to stay there anyway.

Just as Mr. Schust pulled the boat up to the dock, a great swarm of flying insects swooped down on them without warning. It was a sudden and staggering bedlam that should not have been possible from such small things.

Michael could hear his sister shrieking, Mr. Schust cursing, and the figures on the dock calling something out as they waved lanterns to and fro. Michael realized then that the people on the dock were wearing masks on their faces, handkerchiefs wrapped around the backs of their heads like bandits. Behind them was the shadowy hulk of the resort, swaddled in black forest.

Holding his breath so as not to inhale one of the bugs, whose sharp and wriggling bodies kept colliding with his face and tangling in his hair, Michael stood up in the boat and took up his suitcase, wanting to leap to the dock in the hope he might escape the dreadful things.

He heard Mr. Schust shout something, and Frances shriek again as the boat tilted in the water. Undaunted, Michael was about to toss his case onto the dock's wood planks when one of the bugs flew into his ear. A tinny buzzing filled his brain and Michael convulsed sideways, as if the force of his motion would expel the squirming invader.

It didn't, but the violence of the motion sent him

reeling sideways over the edge of the boat. The last thing he heard was everyone in the boat and on the dock shouting all at once, and then he was plunging into the dark, shockingly cold embrace of the lake water. He opened his eyes. There was nothing but a black void around him, and Michael was gripped in a dread feeling when he didn't know which way to swim to get to the surface.

Hearing another splash, Michael was startled, and the breath fled from his lungs as two hands roughly grabbed him around his shoulders. The next moment he was lying on the dock, sputtering up the fetid water, the silhouettes of strangers leaning down over him.

"He's all right," a man's voice said, in a posh accent. "He'll be all right."

Michael blinked water out of his eyes to see a woman who looked remarkably like his mother peering down at him. She had a lantern held up next to her face.

"Mum?" Michael said.

Although he knew it wasn't her, he hoped she would say that yes, she was his mum, and they could just pretend this to be the case for the rest of their lives.

The woman glanced sideways at the bearded man dripping next to her. Michael could already hear the motorboat disappearing back across the lake.

"I'm your Aunt Theresa, sweets. And the damp ogre who just dove in the water to save you is your Uncle Simon."

THE GUEST CHILDREN   21

"Pleased to meet you," Michael said.

Theresa laughed at this, and Simon joined in. His voice was deep and gruff when he spoke. "Apologies for the welcoming committee. They're harmless, those bugs, and only come around now and then. But their numbers can be overwhelming."

"There was one in my ear."

Aunt Theresa took Michael's cold hand in her warm one then. "We'll just have to make sure it's out of there. Right after some hot tea and biscuits, what do you say?"

After Michael was helped up, he accepted a brief embrace from his aunt and a handshake from his uncle. Frances was standing at the foot of the dock, staring off into the forest. The trees there swayed in the breeze, their tips frosted with white moonlight. It was so dark beneath them, a kind of dark so deep even the London blackouts couldn't touch it. Michael didn't like the look of the woods, but chose not to speak his thoughts aloud.

Looking to the big house then, Frances asked, "Is it just you and Uncle Simon here?"

"No," Theresa said, and from the pinched way it came out, Michael knew that his sister had put a foot wrong somehow. He was glad it wasn't him this time.

"We do have some guests at the moment. We've all been so excited to meet you both. We didn't know when you'd arrive, so we've been watching out the windows for days."

Michael followed them along the deck, dripping and

leaving footprints from his sodden shoes. As they moved towards the lodge, he looked to the small strip of beach next to the dock and saw a smashed sandcastle there. He wondered who might have built it, and hoped there might be another boy about, a boy willing to become his friend.

★　★　★

CHAPTER 6

After two weeks in the oppressive quiet of the resort, amidst the whispers and tiptoes of her aunt and uncle and their peculiar guests, Frances was finally able to sleep. She didn't like it here. The forest had them cornered, crowding up on the lodge as if trying to push them off the land and into Blank Lake's dark waters. She didn't like the way the trees looked in through the windows, as if they were observing the lodge's inhabitants like characters in a play.

She'd been awake most nights with a terrible foreboding, even as Michael seemed uncharacteristically gleeful about their new home and the great playground of the forest. He'd been sullen and silent the first few days, but one morning he simply snapped out of it, as though someone had pressed a switch inside him. He entertained Theresa, Simon, and the guests with jokes and exaggerated stories of their voyage. For once, Frances was the troublesome one. She simply couldn't bring herself to pretend that all was well.

That night, Frances woke from dreams of wandering the ruins of London with her brother. Something big stalked them through the rubble, the musical clinking of its footsteps setting her on edge. A terrible rending sound came too, and she saw a barrage balloon torn in half, its slack grey skin spiralling to the ground.

She hurried Michael along, looking for their fireman saviour, or anyone else who might lead them to shelter. The ground shuddered under their feet, but there were no bombers in the sky. The shaking she felt came from those heavy footsteps, and they were getting still nearer. Frances saw a sign for a tube station, the name of it blanked out. She took Michael's hand to lead him there for shelter. When he pulled back against her, not wanting to go, Frances slapped his face. The hurt look Michael gave her struck her right in the tender centre of her heart.

She was trying to save him, why couldn't he see that?

Moving down the steps into the tube tunnel, Frances expected to see light from candles and torches, to hear the voices of adults beckoning the children to join them in safety. But when they got down to the bottom of the steps, there was nothing there. Iron doors slammed behind them, and Frances felt her brother's cold hand snatch at her own.

When Frances awoke that night and opened her eyes in their musty little wallpapered room, there was a boy standing by her bed. His clothes were dripping wet, and his lips were

THE GUEST CHILDREN   25

blue. His face had a swollen look that Frances didn't like. But he had an oddly hopeful expression on his face as he stood next to her.

"May I get into the bed with you?" he said.

He was English, like Frances. His voice had a cold, hollow pitch, like Michael's when he spoke to her from the top of the tubular steel slides at the fairground.

"No, you may not. And I'll thank you to leave my room."

"But I'm quite cold. Just a few moments to warm up, if you don't mind."

"I've already told you that I *do* mind. I don't even know your name."

"My name is Gerald, Miss. I live here like you do. You know my mum and dad. I've been very lonely without any other children around."

"We were told that Cousin Gerald is dead, and I'm going to tell my aunt and uncle that you were bothering me and telling lies."

"Please don't. I'll go. Don't tell them, they'll be cross."

Frances looked across the room then and realized that her brother's bed was empty.

"What have you done with Michael?"

The boy looked down at his feet. A single droplet of water fell from his head. Frances realized he had sand on his bare feet, and all over his body. He'd tracked it across the floor.

"I haven't done anything with him," Gerald said.

Frances leapt out of her bed then. If she'd fooled herself into believing she wasn't frightened, she couldn't do it any longer.

"Where did he go?"

The boy, Gerald, pointed a thin, pale arm out of the window in the direction of the woods. "He's out there now. You might find him, I suppose, if you went out too . . ."

Frances pulled her oversized jumper on over her nightdress and went to get her shoes. Before she went out the door, she said to the boy, "I don't want you to follow me. And I don't want to see you again when we get back. I don't know what you are, but you don't belong here."

★ ★ ★

CHAPTER 7

Earlier that night, Michael heard his name called. At first he ignored it, tried to dampen the voice with the weight of his pillow. When that didn't work, his curiosity overpowered his fear. He climbed out of bed to see who was calling. The voice kept getting farther away, so he had to keep following. He left the room he shared with Frances, went along the hall to the stairs, and down into the dark lobby. Then, crossing through the screened porch, he went into the night.

The night smelled different in this place, nothing at all like home. The air was cleaner, which made it easier to smell the other things, the rotted things and the newly dead things lying in the woods or floating in the water. It wasn't an entirely unpleasant odour, but once Michael had a nose for it, it was practically all he could smell.

Barefoot, though it was October now and the nights were cold, Michael wondered which one of them was calling for him. He couldn't tell from the voice, which sometimes sounded as if it was coming from inside him. Thus far, he'd met the Wet Boy, Mr. Gasmask, and the Red Lady. Sometimes they watched him.

Other times they ignored him altogether. But they never spoke to him. He hadn't yet mustered the courage to try speaking to them first.

But he'd seen other things in the woods too, heard other things saying his name. Tonight, he wasn't sure who was calling him forward. He went along the bumpy path around the back of the lodge and towards the trail leading to Glass Bay. He'd not been there after sunset yet, and knew it was forbidden, but still he pressed on.

Some of the things Michael had seen around the lodge were wondrous. He'd seen a fat red moon almost brushing over the treetops one night. He'd seen pale faces and swift, bony limbs flashing under the surface of Blank Lake. He'd seen trees swaying their branches and sighing like restless human beings. One night he even thought he saw his mum and dad, standing far off on the water and looking back towards the lodge. But, as with the others, there was something warning him not to call out to them.

It was a strange feeling, not wanting to speak to his parents when he'd missed them so. He'd missed their voices and their scents, even their anger, but still he knew this was a rule he should follow, or perhaps he wouldn't get to see them anymore at all.

As Michael tramped along the trail to Glass Bay, he heard something big moving through the damp woods,

THE GUEST CHILDREN 29

shaking rainwater from the trees as it went. It must be a bear, he thought. A great big one, the kind he'd been hoping to see since they arrived, and Frances wouldn't be here. She'd never believe him if she didn't see it with her own eyes.

Michael wasn't afraid, but when he saw what came stepping through the trees to stand before him, he knew something was wrong. He was happy to see his old friend again. But not like this. His size, and the way those bright black eyes of his shone down on him, it wasn't right. And Michael wouldn't have expected him to move on his hind legs the way he did—not big and clumsy like a real bear at all, but almost as fluid and controlled as a man.

"Stanley," he said.

The bear moved up to Michael, then leaned right down and stuck one of those black eyes in his face, like a jeweller examining a precious stone. His breath came in damp, nasal huffs that smelled of the sour sea. It was frightening, and if Michael wasn't too surprised to speak, he would have called out for Frances. But Frances wasn't there to help this time.

So, when his old friend Stanley waved him forward, Michael just did as he was told.

★　★　★

CHAPTER 8

Away from the lodge and the boy who'd called himself Gerald, Frances stepped over a felled tree, hearing Michael's voice ahead. There was a light rain, and the sheets of stone on the forest floor were slick and slippery. She wished she'd brought an umbrella. Frances moved as quietly as she could manage, but it was hard going. When she got closer, Frances could see who Michael was speaking to. It frightened her so much that she gasped out loud.

Stanley. Tatty old Stanley. Michael's stuffed bear, lost at sea weeks before.

But Stanley was as tall as a man now, and dripping wet with sea water, with kelp and other green things all hanging off him. When Frances let out a gasp, Stanley turned to her, his head swivelling unnaturally backwards to look where she stood. He had the most awfully empty black eyes. Those eyes gazed right into her, and she knew then that it wasn't really Stanley—it was that awful boy from her room, Gerald. Frances felt the night air drawing into her

THE GUEST CHILDREN 31

lungs for a scream, but then it was snatched away and she couldn't find her breath at all.

Gazing upwards at the huge bear, Michael had the broadest, most artificial smile on his face, like the forced grin he gave when they had to pose for a photograph.

"Michael . . ." Frances said. "I think you should come back now."

Michael's eyes were wide when he spoke, his voice high and strained. "Look who I found," he said. "It's jolly old Stambly, back from the sea."

"That's not Stanley," Frances said.

Stanley shook his head then. It was such a faint motion that Frances could barely make it out, and she couldn't tell what it meant. Was he agreeing, or warning her to be silent?

"Frances," Michael said. "Stanley tells me that he can show us something wonderful. It's just a little further along into the woods."

Frances was drawn into those black eyes staring back into her. It gave her a queasy feeling, like looking down from a great height, or into the deep dark of an old well. She felt in her stomach that she had to be very careful about what she said next. Her heart was skittering and her mouth dry as she gathered herself to answer her brother.

"Aunt Theresa says it's time for us to get back into bed. She's quite upset that we're up and about, and we simply must go back now. Perhaps you could tell Stanley that we might join him tomorrow?"

Before she'd even finished speaking, Stanley leaned down

over Michael. A piece of seaweed fell off him and slithered down Michael's face as Stanley whispered something in his ear. But it wasn't whispering, not really, because Stanley didn't have a mouth, just a jagged line of loose, damp stitching that looked as if it was coming apart.

"Stanley says Theresa is sleeping. She doesn't mind. Stanley says to come."

Stanley put a big paw over Michael's shoulder and started guiding him deeper into the woods. Frances followed, not because she wanted to, but because she knew that if she ran back for Aunt Theresa, she'd never see her brother again.

She spoke to Michael's back as he walked in front of her. "Don't you remember, Michael? Simon told us we mustn't come out here, and we mustn't speak to anyone. No one at all. As we're their guests, we're obliged to obey their rules, don't you agree?"

Michael looked back but said nothing. Stanley continued to urge him forward, his big wet stuffed feet barely making a sound on the forest floor.

"That's what Mum and Dad would've wanted us to do, after all. To be good."

"Stanley's taking us to Mum and Dad right now, Frances."

Michael's voice cracked when he said that, and Frances was certain he was crying. She followed, and Stanley waited for her to catch up. He made her hold out her hand, and when she did, he swallowed it up in his damp, sandy paw.

THE GUEST CHILDREN 33

Frances thought she could feel things moving inside the paw, squirming and wriggling things inside the stuffing.

"I think we should go back now," she said.

Neither Stanley nor Michael answered her, they only moved on through the dark. As they walked farther along the overgrown trail, low-hanging branches whispered off Stanley's hide. Frances could just see through the trees to the dark, wet finger of Glass Bay to her right. She was afraid now. Her legs trembled so fiercely she could scarcely put one foot in front of the other.

She wished she'd never left her bed.

They came to the top of the steep outcropping of rock overlooking the beach. The sign there that read *To Glass Bay* looked as though it was painted a very long time ago. There was a wooden staircase clinging to the face of the dark rock, one they'd gone up and down despite being warned away. The stairs shook now with the motion of someone climbing them. Beyond the steps, Frances saw the shoddy wooden playhouse on the bayshore called the Sand Palace. Then she saw an impossible thing, a thing that made her take a step back and away.

The people climbing the stairs were her mum and dad.

They looked as they did on the night they died, Mum in her dressing gown and Dad in his nightshirt, broken glasses hanging off one ear. They were dusty and dead, just as they were before Frances pulled Michael out of the house and into the street.

When her parents reached the top of the stairs, Dad

walking funny on one leg, Stanley went to stand with them and opened his arms, like a showman with a curtain rising behind him. Mum and Dad were smiling, but Frances didn't want to see them like that. Turning away, she heard their footsteps thumping and shuffling closer. She looked to Stanley, but the bear wasn't there anymore, it was just the boy. Thin, blue-lipped Gerald looked back at her, wide-eyed and shivering, with an expression she couldn't read. Frances took Michael's hand and closed her eyes so she could stop looking.

"It's not them," Michael hissed. "But we must pretend it is, Frances. We must."

★ ★ ★

PART 2

TO BLANK LAKE

CHAPTER 9

The end of the war nearly ended my life. Thousands of miles from the last of the fighting, we were just about through hoisting a roof piece atop one of the Victory Houses at the new Queensway Park site. The piece was so heavy that all seven of us were grunting from the chore, wishing for more hands. It was one of the two-storey models, always a harder go than the smaller ones. With ropes and all the muscle we could spare, we just about had the thing secured in place when some fool came dancing across the pockmarked farmland, hollering about victory.

I'd have been as happy about the news as the next man, happier still if you want to know the truth, but Lou Clark, poised on a ladder at the roof peak, threw up his hands with witless joy and let go of the frame. The other man up top tried to hang on, but he didn't have the strength, and all that heavy lumber came sliding down right on top of me.

Everyone was shouting now, some about the frame and

others about the surrender. Me, I was diving out of the way. The lumber glanced off my shoulder and sent me face-first into the dust, knocking the wind from my lungs. Another inch and it would've broken my shoulder. A couple more, it would've broken my neck.

Clarence came out of the workshop already bellowing about the commotion. He saw the cracked frame in the dirt and me rising from the ground, gripping my shoulder. Lou was down the ladder by then, leaping about like a spooked horse and flailing his arms. I took a step towards him, but Clarence put a sweaty hand on my chest before I could get there and asked everyone what the hell was going on.

Even Clarence couldn't stay sore when he heard the news. After the bombs fell, we knew the surrender was coming, but it was another thing to hear it said out loud after all those years, and all those dead, and all the rest of it.

He wasn't about to start jumping around like Lou and some of the others, but Clarence did light a half-cigar from his soot-stained shirt pocket. A smile cracked his broad, sunburnt face. I was glowering at Lou, my left hand balled up, but I couldn't stay mean with all that jubilation surrounding me. Clarence let it go on for another minute, and then he said, "End of the war means more of those boys are coming home, and they're gonna need houses. I'm not gonna be the one to tell 'em they aren't ready, how about you?"

It took another minute of fading whoops and cheers,

THE GUEST CHILDREN 39

but the men soon all calmed down and got back to it. I saw Lou sneaking a nip from his dented nickel hip flask, so I told Clarence not to let him up any more ladders and put him on digging post holes down the road. Get him far away from me, was the point I wanted to get across. Clarence nodded, stubbed out his cigar, and went to grab Lou by the collar. I'm not sure Lou ever even knew what he did wrong.

The house we were putting together would be insulated with rockwool and tarpaper before the sun went down. The walls would go in, and then the paint men would come along with their sprayers and the roofers would slap shingles overtop. By then, we'd be well under way on the framing for the next one.

Thirty-six hours to build a house when it went right, and most of the time it did. They weren't meant to last long, but they were still far better places to live than the one-room dump I shared with my younger brother, Edward.

My shift ended just before nightfall. When I was done, I shuffled out through the dirt with the rest of the men. My shoulder ached, and the rest of me wasn't faring much better. The pace of the work seemed to get quicker every day, with Clarence cracking the whip and threatening to replace us in that sticky August heat—especially when the architects were there from Wartime Housing, their skinny white arms showing under the short sleeves of those camel-coloured smocks.

40 Patrick Tarr

I walked out towards the Queensway, the long hike to the Long Branch loop to get the streetcar to the Roncesvalles loop, and then a switch to another car along Queen Street to home. As I went, I passed a steam shovel motoring along, its long black arm and claw dangling uselessly in the dust-fogged twilight. The other men talked and laughed and celebrated the end of the war. I was happy too, but as usual, I walked on my own. Just like I ate lunch on my own and went and sat on my own during smoke and coffee breaks. I didn't have too much to say to the rest of them, so it was better to keep a distance.

The streetcars were both crowded when I boarded. It only got worse closer to home. There was a victory celebration starting around University Avenue and it seemed as though the whole city was on its way. There were families with children, veterans in uniform, and older couples dressed up like they were going to Sunday service. A group of young women, factory girls by the looks of them, got on and wedged in with the crowd, everyone leaning and swaying as one as the car got up to speed on the tracks. I was crammed in at the back, in need of a wash and a change of clothes. My shoulder ached, and I kept seeing flashes of that roof piece sliding down at me.

One of the factory girls kept looking in my direction, and only then did I really notice her. I tried not to flinch when I saw who it was, but I don't think I did a very good job of it. Mildred whispered something to her friends, made

THE GUEST CHILDREN

a show of steeling herself, then walked back to where I stood near the rear doors of the car. Crowded as it was, people still made way for Mildred. She always had that strange, undefinable quality that made strangers their best selves in her presence. It wasn't a quality that I shared.

"Hello Rand," she said.

"Mildred." I think she expected me to say more, but I left it at that.

"How are you? I've been assembling rifles, if you can believe that."

"I do believe it. I'm sure yours shoot the straightest of them all."

"Is that supposed to be funny?"

"No. Just saying you never did anything halfway."

"You say that like there's something wrong with it."

"Not at all."

Nothing I could say to Mildred was likely to change her opinion of me, so I wasn't about to waste a lot of words trying.

"I don't suppose you heard about my James," she said. "He died in Italy. Killed by a sniper, they said. He'd only just arrived. I never even got a letter."

"I'm sorry to hear that."

"We had a few days together after the wedding. That was our whole marriage. Then he shipped out, and I never saw him again."

"I'm sure he was a brave man."

42 Patrick Tarr

"You were one of the lucky ones, weren't you. You and Edward both." I could tell some other passengers were eavesdropping by now.

"I know."

Mildred's look softened then, but more in pity than with any residue of affection. "So, how is your brother doing these days?"

"No better. Probably a little worse with the war going on so long. He's not able to work anymore. And there's no one else to look after him. Only me. But I did what I could to pitch in, building those Victory Houses and whatnot for soldiers coming home."

I hated the plaintive tone I could hear in my own voice. I knew it wouldn't make any difference. I'd been here before. Her mind was already made up. I could see that people around us had sensed a shift, a change in the air. More of them were watching now. Mildred looked back to her friends, who were eyeing us from down the car. The driver slowed abruptly, and when I bumped into her, she looked annoyed.

"Heading down for the celebration, are you?"

She nodded. "I don't suppose you're going down too."

"I'm afraid I can't."

"Just as well."

"I hope you have a good time. And again, my condolences."

"Say hello to your brother, Rand."

With this, Mildred smiled tightly, and pinned me with

THE GUEST CHILDREN   43

a green-eyed stare. She turned and walked down the car without another word. I could see the slight shake of her head as she went.

All eyes were on me now. The car came to its shuddering halt at the next stop and I slipped through a gap in the passengers, out onto the street. As the car pulled away, I looked to the window and saw Mildred and her friends all watching me through the glass.

It was a bad feeling, the way they were looking. No matter how many times I got that look, it stuck me in a place that drew blood. I hoped the end of the war would mean the end of all that, but I stood there and let them ogle me until the streetcar finally rumbled them all away to their party. It was my way of showing them I wasn't ashamed. Because I wasn't.

I'd done what I had to do.

★   ★   ★

Chapter 10

When I got to the building where I lived with my brother, some of our neighbours were hanging out of windows and cheering. Others were drinking and milling about on the sidewalk or in doorways. There was some dancing, and some weeping. I wanted to be happy with them, to join in and drink beer and sing songs. But I was worried about what all this noise had done to Edward. I knew he'd be in a state, and I'd have some work ahead before he'd calm down.

I ducked down the alley and went up through the back door, as I usually did. In our second-floor hallway, the air was laden with cigarette smoke and the rumblings of voices from other apartments. When I got to our door, I did the secret knock.

Rap, tap tap, rap rap.

After a moment I heard Edward whisper my name through the door. "Rand . . . ?"

"Yes," I said. "It's Randall."

THE GUEST CHILDREN

"I don't believe you."

"Just move the dresser, would you?"

I heard the dresser dragged from in front of the door. There wasn't any more noise after that, so he was going to make me do the rest.

Sighing, I pulled out my keys, the movement making my shoulder throb. Once I'd opened the door, I saw Edward's shape huddled in the far corner. It was near black inside, with no lights on and all the windows papered over. I struck a match from the box by the door and my brother's pale face lit up, along with the blade of the kitchen knife held out in front of him.

"They've come, haven't they." His voice was high-pitched and tight, and I knew he was in a bad way, even for him.

"Didn't you hear, Edward? The war is over."

"No," he said. "No, it isn't. I can hear the screaming."

"It's shouting, not screaming. Celebrating, you understand? The Germans surrendered ages ago. The Japanese surrendered today. It's done now. Nobody's coming."

I could tell he wanted to believe me. Moving to him, I put my hands on his shoulders and felt him shudder. "You must be hungry."

After Edward and I ate tinned soup and crackers at our crooked little card table in the cramped room, we talked about what it all meant for us. It seemed the Victory House projects would be going on for some time, if not at Queensway Park, then on some other tract of old farmland around the city. I was hopeful there'd be enough work coming that we wouldn't have to build another shack down in the valley. Even this dim, dingy closet was better than that.

I tried to keep my brother focused on the future, the next steps. Edward was at his best when I kept him in a narrow view of things, but he was too excited that night. He still thought the end of the war could be a lie, a test of our loyalty and perseverance. He'd long been certain the Germans were going to come for us, iron-eyed soldiers pinwheeling out of the sky under blood-red parachutes. It's why we lived the way we did, as if we were holed up on the ragged edge of the front, not safe in the middle of a city thousands of miles from the war.

I tried to ease Edward out of his loping panic, as I always did, but he'd spent his time drinking too much coffee cut with the cheap whiskey I'd rationed out to him for the long day without me. The two things together put him into a state of clench-jawed near panic. I knew I shouldn't leave him with either, but I'd tried that, and it just made him worse.

When I told him I'd seen Mildred on the streetcar, Edward went quiet for a while. I wanted him to say something to make me feel better about it. After all, that was what I did for him most of the time, asking nothing in return.

Finally, he said, "She was no good for you. She didn't see how things have to be. You're better off, really you are."

"I'm not sure that's true, Edward."

THE GUEST CHILDREN

"*I'm* sure. And I can see more clearly than you, Rand. I always have."

I could have spent some time arguing that with him, but there was no point. After a while, I left my brother to peer out the peepholes in the window paper and went to my cot to try to get some sleep before my next shift. It was stuffy with all the windows nailed shut, and I was sweating on the narrow mattress even with my shirt off and the covers stripped away. I'd always been able to sleep through anything, even Edward's pacing and muttering, but my shoulder was still hurting me, and I couldn't make myself cross over.

I rolled to my other side and looked at the peeling paint on the wall. Blinking a few times, I was right on the edge of drifting away, but then I remembered the sight of Mildred and her friends looking down on me from that streetcar, and it chased away any chance of sleep for good. No matter what I told myself, those looks still got under my skin sometimes. And with Mildred, there was that ache in me for what I'd lost those years ago.

Memories of her often took hold of me in the fragile last moments of the day. The feelings had dulled over time, but they came back now, sharp and astringent as alcohol on a fresh scrape. I'd wanted to enlist since 1940, and I was keen again to go in right after Normandy, when they needed new recruits. But with Edward growing worse as the war raged on, I couldn't leave him alone for more than a ten-hour shift. I surely couldn't put him back in a hospital after his first turn. He'd left our room alone one day and gotten into a fight, breaking one man's nose and biting another clean through his hand. The raging, wild-eyed state of him when I'd fished him out of that ward was something I'd never forget. He couldn't be helped in those places. Hard as he was to abide most of the time, I loved my brother, and he belonged with me.

I looked at him now, peering out of a slit in the papered-over window, and missed the brave, wild boy he used to be. What Edward had become as a grown man was at least partly my fault, so he was my burden to carry.

Still suffering from the heat, I went to the tiny kitchen sink and rinsed my face and arms with a cold cloth. I looked at myself in the mirror, but I couldn't stand to do it for long. I could see Edward watching me now from the table behind me—that thinner, graver, unshaven version of my face, his black hair roughly chopped by my hand, like mine was done by his.

Even in my reflection, I couldn't be alone. Not that alone was what I wanted, not really. Anyway, there was nothing to be done about it. As I went back to lie down, my guts went tight at the thought of the life before me.

Edward ticked off the seconds of my wakefulness as he got up and paced the floor.

★ ★ ★

CHAPTER 11

Most nights, I fought a war in my dreams that I'd dodged in real life. Wherever I was, some grim and cratered beach of coiled barbed wire and blood-tinged waves, the battle was already over. Scores of dead men lay scattered across the sand and floating in the shallow water. Apart from me, there was not a living soul, although I often felt some presence watching me.

In these dreams, I was searching for someone. Sometimes it was our mother, a woman I didn't remember and whose name I didn't even know. She had no place being on this beach, and was likely long dead, but she needed finding all the same. Other times, I was searching for Mildred. Those dreams began after she abruptly broke off our engagement and married someone else. When my thoughts of her tapered off over time, the dreams about her did too.

Most often, in these dreams, I was looking for Edward. But on the night the war ended, it was different. For once, I wasn't looking for anything. As always, my only company

50 Patrick Tarr

on the bleak, imagined beach were the scores of dead. Their faces were mercifully turned away from me, as clouds of dust and the smoke from burning vehicles roiled across the beach. I couldn't see much beyond my own searching hands in front of me, but I heard someone call out my name. Blinded as I was, I staggered into a yawning crater in the sand, tumbling down into red water.

The smoke crept over the hole, but as I tried to clamber my way back up to the beach, it was as though that smoke turned solid, becoming a ceiling of veiny grey glass. I thought I saw someone standing over the hole, looking down on me. I pounded and pounded, screaming for help, but the glass wouldn't break. The damp sand walls of the crater started to collapse in clumps around me, rising from my feet until it reached my neck.

I woke up then, pounding my fist on the peeling plaster wall next to my cot. Edward was sitting at the card table, drinking and watching me. The air was choked with his cigarette smoke. He stubbed one out and sipped from his mug.

"Where were you?"

"Far."

"Was it good?"

"Not so good, no."

"I'm sorry, Rand."

"It's not your fault I have bad dreams."

This wasn't entirely true, but Edward nodded and came

to sit on the edge of my cot. He put his hand on my head. It was cool. He flattened my sweaty hair and sighed.

"I'll read to you if you like," he said.

Edward seemed to have exhausted himself of his anxiety. He went to fetch one of the books we kept on a tiny shelf in the corner. I saw which book it was. It had come across the Atlantic with us when we were sent to Canada as boys. *Five Children and It.*

Edward started reading. I took a cigarette and some whiskey and lay there listening until I fell asleep again.

The last thing I remember him saying was, "*They didn't know being dead is only being asleep, and you're bound to wake up somewhere or other, either where you go to sleep or some better place.*" His voice got quieter and quieter, until I couldn't hear him at all.

The next morning, I heard about the prime minister's end-of-war holiday declaration over the radio and went back to sleep for a while in the dim haze of our room. I'm not sure that Edward slept at all. When I rolled out of my cot, groggy and still sore in the shoulder, I went to where Edward sat by the window and took his coffee out of his hand to have a sip. There was whiskey in it, of course, but I said nothing about it, and neither did he.

Already, I could hear the shouts and cheers of people celebrating on the street. I still wanted to go out and join them, to feel a bit of life around me, the press and smell of other bodies up close, but I knew this would be a bad day for Edward. I'd have to settle for watching through the peepholes in the window. We did that for a while in silence, as chattering mobs ambled past on their way to City Hall. I turned on the radio after that, but I could tell it was putting Edward on edge, so I turned it off again. I was just getting around to taking a walk when we heard footsteps in the hallway, and the thump of a fist on our door.

Edward stared at me, wide-eyed, lowering his voice to a hiss. "Don't," he said.

I was growing tired of him already. It would be a long day. Just to get a rise out of him, I walked to the door with my hand reaching out towards the knob. My brother leapt up in a panic, his hand reaching out for the kitchen knife he'd left on the table.

"I was only teasing," I whispered. "Go hide in the closet, why don't you . . ."

Edward stepped away from the door as whoever was on the other side thumped again, a little harder this time. A woman's voice said, "You got a telephone call downstairs."

It was Sybil, our neighbour. I wanted to open up to say thanks, but I couldn't do that with Edward standing there. I just expressed my gratitude through the door and told her I'd be down in a minute. Once I heard her footsteps go back down the hall, I looked at him.

"Who's calling?" he asked.

"How would I know?"

"People don't just *call* you, Rand."

"All the more reason to see what it's all about."

THE GUEST CHILDREN 53

Edward shrank back as I opened the door, and I heard him hurry to lock it behind me before I even got to the stairs. Down there in the little telephone cupboard, I picked the receiver up off the desk. I knew who it was before I even heard him speak, from the quick and impatient breathing over the line.

"Randall. It's Clarence. I'm calling with some hard news."

"Hard for who?"

"I gotta let you go. Can't use you at the site anymore. There's men coming back who need work, and I'm told I'm to hire them. You're a good worker, but that's how it is."

"What about all the money I've been kicking back to you?"

"I earned it."

Then Clarence hung up, and I was out of a job.

Stung from the news, I took my time getting back to Edward, heading outside to loop around a few blocks first. It was a lot to think about. Finding the job hadn't been easy. I'd had to tithe back a piece of my wages to Clarence as a bribe for giving me the work, so we had nothing saved. With no money coming in, we'd miss next month's rent and be back on the street.

When I got back up to the second-floor corridor, there was a man in uniform with our neighbour, Sybil. They were pressed against the wall, kissing and carrying on. His hand slid up her leg and inside her skirt as I stood there. They hadn't heard me yet, but I knew they would if I had to knock at the door and wait for Edward to open, so I went out again, to the back stairs.

I climbed over the railing to rap on the window. I saw Edward's eye press against the peephole in the paper. His voice was muffled when he spoke.

"What are you doing out there?"

"Just open the window and get out of the way, Edward, for God's sake."

I had to jump from the steps and hang on to the window ledge, pulling myself up so I could wriggle my way through. I didn't care for heights and didn't like risking my neck after my close call at the site the day before. My brother was hunched down in the corner as he watched me tumble to the floor, his fists balled in front of his face. I went to my cot and lay down for a minute. Edward wanted me to go out into the hall and shoo Sybil and her soldier away, but I told him that if it troubled him so much, he could go out and tell them himself.

In truth I was more than happy to keep talking about Sybil, because it delayed me having to tell Edward I was out of work. He told me what he'd heard on the radio and what he'd seen out the window while I was gone.

"Where did you go?" he said.

"Just for a walk."

"Who was on the phone? Something happened, I can tell."

He'd know if I was lying, so I just came out with it. "I lost my job, Edward."

THE GUEST CHILDREN

Edward took it hard, jumping up and pacing the little room. He kept repeating that we couldn't go back to living out of doors again. He was right, just not for the reasons he gave. I wasn't sure we'd survive another winter of it, especially with no money for food.

"What are we going to do, Rand?"

"You mean, what am *I* going to do," I said.

"We're in it together, don't pretend we aren't."

"I'll find something soon, all right?"

"You'd better. If we have to leave here, I think I'll die."

★ ★ ★

Chapter 12

I found something.

It would only be temporary work, but the pay was good, and it would give me some time out of town, away from Edward for a spell. I jumped at the chance. Three days after I lost my building job, I walked out of the apartment on my way to catch a northbound train. I heard the dresser slide into place as I turned the door locks behind me. Edward had his tinned ham and crackers, apples, and some limp vegetables I'd bought at a discount from the greengrocer down the street. Enough to keep him for a week.

When I went down the stairs, my suitcase thumped against my leg. It felt good to be going somewhere. It was ages since I'd been anywhere but to work, much longer since I'd felt free of my brother. When I got down to the street, I was sure I could see him peering through the peephole in the upper window, his eye a dark jewel shining from behind the newspaper.

After a long walk winding through side streets to avoid

The Guest Children

crowds, I came to Union Station. Inside, it was a tumult of people, carts, and steamer trunks. I felt my suitcase pressing against my chest before I realized I'd heaved it up there, like a shield. There were men in uniform all around, some reuniting with their girls and others with their families.

I could see a dividing line running through these men just by looking at their faces. There were some who I'm sure looked rather like me. These were the men who'd missed out on the whole affair, or the ones who'd joined up but avoided shipping out overseas—"zombies," as some called them. And then there were the others. Those coming back from the war. There was a difference in their faces. The way their eyes took in the world gave them away.

One of these men stood at the end of the platform where I went to wait for my train. Dressed in the blue serge of the RCAF, he had his suitcase in one hand and a cane in the other. From the way he held himself, it looked as if he was in some pain. His face had a puffed, red look and was criss-crossed with scars. Some of his ear was gone, too, but his blue eyes, a shade lighter than the uniform, blazed with unsettling intensity.

At first, I thought he was staring at me, even assessing me, but maybe that was only my own conscience. Whatever he was thinking, when a train whistled its departure, it startled me so much that I nearly dropped my suitcase. The airman didn't even blink. I turned away from him, thinking about the journey and the task ahead.

I'd found the job in the back listings of a newspaper I

58

Patrick Tarr

pulled out of the trash can outside our building. The first few calls I made looking for work all went the same way. The moment they asked if I was just coming home from serving overseas, it was all over.

But next to the job listings, I saw something else.

It was a small piece about two orphaned children from London, Frances and Michael Hawksby, who'd gone missing in the wilds north of the city sometime in late 1940. They'd been meant to stay with relatives to ride out the war, but there'd been no word of them since they'd arrived in Canada, and their extended family in England was worried. There was an address and a phone number listed for anyone to call with information on their whereabouts.

The story got me thinking. The closest town to where they'd vanished was Creekmont, which itself wasn't too far from where Edward and I had grown up on the Sturgess farm. Not to mention, before the war, I'd put in some time as a night watchman for a security agency, and I might be able to exaggerate my bona fides enough to convince these people to pay me as something like a private detective. I figured I could suggest that they hire me to look around the area, promising to find out where the Hawksby children were, even if it was in a grave.

There was more to my interest than that, though I'm not sure I had a conscious sense of it until later. These lost children reminded me of things I'd tried to leave behind long ago. I believed then that my reasons for taking on the task of finding the Hawksby children were all practical, but

The Guest Children

in truth, even as I tried to get away from Edward, I was taking myself back to the landscapes and memories of our childhood. I might as well have packed him with my things.

I spoke with a secretary through the number in the paper and managed to get to her employer, landing on a man with a voice like a muted tuba. I must've made a pretty good case for myself as an investigator, because he agreed to meet with me the next day. That morning, I smoothed down my hair and did my best to press my jacket and some trousers for the meeting, sneaking out while Edward slept. At a building just off University Avenue, I was ushered into a wood-panelled office to meet a silver-haired man with the same voice I'd heard on the phone. His eyes were light brown, like his suit, and bloodshot in the way of a heavy drinker. He regarded me, blinking, until I asked him for more information about Frances and Michael Hawksby.

He told me the children were shipped over in the fall of 1940, after the bombing deaths of their parents during the early days of the Blitz. They were meant to stay with an aunt and uncle, but any records of their names and addresses had somehow been lost. The fact that the aunt and uncle owned a resort on or near some place called Blank Lake was all he had for me.

Using some inside lingo I remembered from my time working in security, I convinced the man he'd be better off with me looking into things than with some bigger outfit. I was cheaper, and I knew the area. But I don't think he cared so much about the children as he did about proving to the family in England that he was doing something with their money.

After we agreed on terms, I asked for an advance on expenses. He promised to wire money to Creekmont if I could pay my own train fare to get up there. I'd take the train north from the city the next day, and be paid ten dollars a day, which was a sight better than what I got building houses. He stood up to shake my hand. I could feel his eyes on me and knew the question he was going to ask before he asked it.

"You been over there?"

"Family matters kept me back."

"Well," he said. "These children survived the Blitz, and the bomb that killed their parents. They lived through crossing the Atlantic in '40, with U-boats and God knows what else trying to put them in their graves. Consider yourself lucky that they'll be as close to the war as you ever had to get."

When I got back to the apartment, I thought Edward would be excited by the news, but he wasn't. He was happy to have me bringing in money, but he didn't want me to leave town—especially where I was going. Because so many bad things happened to us around there when we were boys, he was convinced it was a bad place. I tried to tell him I'd only be gone a few days, maybe a week, and that we had no other choice if we wanted to keep our room beyond the end of the month, but he kept telling me it would be the end of us. Finally, in the face of my determination, he relented, and told me to do what I liked.

I watched Edward for a minute, thinking he was just hanging his head in a sulk, before I realized he was looking at something on the floor. Whatever it was, he peered at it from one angle then another. It was like he'd forgotten I was there.

"What are you looking at?"

"There's sand," he said.

"What sand?"

"On the floor. Don't you see it?"

"I just carried it in on my boots from outdoors, Edward. I can sweep it up."

The look he gave me then was so strange—like a parent talking to a small child, explaining that the way they saw something in the world was plain wrong.

"No, Rand, you can't."

★ ★ ★

CHAPTER 13

The climb onto the train and the journey to my seat was a crush of coats, cases, handbags, and umbrellas. I wasn't accustomed to the scents of perfume and cologne, and my eyes stung as I passed through clouds of both on my way down the aisle, slipping and bumping through a line of people stowing luggage overhead. I took my place without meeting anyone's gaze.

When I sank into my seat, the soft hiss of it accepting my weight, the noise around me fell into a hush. Staring out the window at the comings and goings of other passengers, I could feel a difference in the air. For all the optimism and celebration, there was an uncertainty too. I imagined that some were wondering, as I was, if the good news could be real. The stain of all the things we'd seen and heard on newsreels and the radio didn't simply wash out in a day.

Shortly after we pulled out of the station, the rocking motion of the train coaxed me into a restless sleep. By the

THE GUEST CHILDREN

time we were out of the city, I was pulled under. At the beginning, I held on to a vague sense of what was going on around me. There was still the feeling of a rolling party in the passenger car. Although it was early yet, I could smell liquor, even over the thickening haze of cigarette and pipe smoke. A woman laughed. Two men engaged in some quiet squabble. A trolley clattered past, striking a seat.

After a little while, all that faded and shifted too. Then there were crickets around me, the gasps of windblown trees, and the rattle of loose shutters Mr. Sturgess never had time to fix. I didn't want to be back there on the farm, had vowed with Edward never to return, but the place was conjured into my thoughts again the moment I saw the piece about the missing children. So there I was, under the clothesline, looking up towards our old bedroom window.

I had no memories of our real parents, and I couldn't remember anything at all from our life in London, where we were told we were born. Our father died in the Great War, according to Mrs. Sturgess, the woman who took us in after we got snatched up by the Fairbridge Society and carried off to Canada. We weren't the only ones like that. Tens of thousands of orphans or paupers like us were pulled from destitution and sent to the colonies to find purpose in labour.

Mrs. Sturgess fed and clothed us while her husband made us work ourselves to the point of exhaustion before and after school. The Sturgess farm raised dairy cows, chickens, potatoes, and carrots. Years after we fled the place, I remembered the long days of work, but couldn't even remember our adoptive parents' Christian names.

Mrs. Sturgess told us that our mother was a godless woman, unfit to raise children, and that we were living in squalid conditions before our salvation. It's something you'd think I might remember. We arrived in Ontario in 1922, when I was six and my brother was five. My memories begin somewhere around that time, and Edward is central to all of them. I never felt love for Mr. or Mrs. Sturgess, but for my brother I would have done anything.

When we arrived, it was the autumn of the Great Fire. We weren't far from where it burned. The skies were a burnt-orange haze of sunlight choked with smoke. The smell burned my eyes and nose whenever we were outside, which was most of the time. I feared I'd look out our grimy bedroom window to see those trees in a curtain of flame, but the fire never got that close.

Our school was a tiny red-brick building with just a handful of children, most of them older than my brother and me. Edward was a strange boy, always strange, so the other boys wanted to take a poke at him a lot of the time. As his older brother, I tried to stop it, for better or worse. We were always outnumbered. Most of these scuffles ended with us both taking a beating. The funny thing about Edward was, he never cried. Not once. Back then, he was defiant.

As I looked up at the house, a young Edward ran past me. I had no choice but to follow. We ran, the two of us,

The Guest Children 65

away from the shouts of Mr. Sturgess into the tangle of woods bordering the property, and the little shack we'd built as our hideout. We needed a place to be safe, but escaping Mr. Sturgess was only ever a temporary measure. The beating we took for running off into the forest was worse than the one we'd take if we didn't, but we always chose to run from him anyway. It was a lesson we simply never learned.

We followed the winding path we'd struck through the tall forest of black spruce, Jack pine, poplar, and birch. We'd found clever ways to make our tracks disappear here and there, leapfrogging over rocks or swinging from low branches so there wasn't an easy trail for Mr. Sturgess to follow if he came looking.

Sometimes he did come looking. Other times he just went back to work and waited to drag us to the woodshed when we got back, his belt already hanging over the swell of his sunburned forearm.

It was quiet in the woods that afternoon, one of those grey autumn days when it's not raining but there's so much damp in the air that it might as well. We were dressed too lightly, in trousers with cotton shirts on top, already wet from the drippings of the tree canopy overhead and the shrubs we ducked through as we followed our secret path. For some reason, we never spoke on our journey to the shack, as if in doing so we'd give away our secret.

After a few minutes, we reached the little hollow where we'd built the shack. It was made from scrap lumber we'd found on the farm and at the roadside, along with some deadfall and whatever else we could scrounge to make the thing stand up and shelter us from the worst of the weather. It was the only thing we had that was ours, and we loved it. Sometimes we played games like conkers in there, my string of chestnuts reigning undefeated, but most often we just sat, grateful for the reprieve from the farmhouse.

When we saw our shack, we knew something wasn't right. We hadn't left any empty liquor bottles outside—that we both knew for sure. We could also see some ratty old trousers put out to dry on the roof and then left out through the night's downpour.

"Someone's in there," I said, in the whisper we used after lights out.

Edward had a sly look in his eye. "Go and look, will you?"

"I'm not going to look."

"We'll go together, then."

"Edward, no."

Edward smirked, a habit of his that often got him in trouble with Mr. and Mrs. Sturgess. He yanked my arm and we crept forward, moving silently through the mist. As we drew nearer, I thought I could hear breathing inside, the heavy rasp of a sleeping man. When we got close to the opening, I smelled stale urine, and the sour musk of an unwashed body.

We peered inside, and sure enough there was a man in there. We couldn't see his face, but I saw the filthy lump of him clear enough, taking up most of the structure. His hairy bare legs lay across my collection of stones and old animal bones from the forest. I wanted to get out of there right away, but Edward got that look again.

"It's *our* shack," he whispered. "We gotta get him out."

"How?"

Before he could answer, the man let out a great, rattling cough and spit onto the dirt floor of our shack. It startled me enough that I cried out and fell onto my back. When I looked back through the door of the shed, there was a dirty, bearded face peering out. The man's blue eyes were fixed on me, and he started crawling out of the shed towards us.

"Who in de fuck are you?" he said, his voice a wet wheeze.

"That's our shack," I said, skittering backwards across dead leaves on my palms and heels. I looked to Edward, but he'd vanished. Alone with the man now, fear knotted up my belly. "We didn't know you were here."

There was a clink as he crawled over a bottle. He snatched it up and held it out in front of him. Scrambling to my feet, I continued to retreat from the man, but kept an eye on him as I did. I thought I could outrun the man easily, but I didn't want to turn my back to him.

I'd just bumped into a tree trunk when Edward leapt out from behind the shack between the man and me and swung a heavy length of dead branch. He was only eleven then, so not in possession of great strength, but still the man's head spun sideways from the force of the blow as he fell to the dirt. Edward let out a whoop as the man roared in pain, and stood over his fallen form with the branch held aloft.

I ran.

Up over the rise of the hollow and through the woods, branches whipping my face as I leapt over fallen trees and stones. It was a good twenty strides before I realized I didn't hear Edward's footsteps behind me. Instead, I heard him cry out in pain back by the shack. Part of me wanted to keep going, far away from the sight and smell of that horrible man. But I'd sworn to stick with my brother no matter what, so I turned around and went back for him.

When I got there, the man had Edward pinned on the ground, one hand around his neck and the other pulling at his hair. Edward had blood all over his face, but it wasn't all his own—some of it was dripping from a jagged wound in the man's scalp where Edward had struck him. The man grunted and cursed in some foreign language. Edward wasn't making a sound, because his windpipe was choked off. There was a funny look in his eyes and a deep cut along his hairline where he'd taken a blow from the broken bottle lying next to the man's hand.

Edward looked at me creeping towards them, holding my eye as I drew up. I got close, but the man still didn't know I was there as he grunted and wheezed, trying to kill my brother with his bare hands, choking him with one and punching him with the other. I could see Edward's eyes bulging out, the fine vessels ruptured inside and turning

The Guest Children

the whites to red. Edward's legs were kicking and scraping the dirt. He was growing weaker by the moment.

The branch Edward used on the man was just lying there, so I picked it up. I closed my hands around the rough bark and felt the weight, thinking about where I should hit the man to buy us enough time to run away. I was still deciding that when Mr. Sturgess came charging down into the hollow. There was a roar in his throat. I'd never seen the man move so fast.

He had a hatchet with him, and he swung it crossways without breaking stride, knocking the man clear off Edward and into the brush. The man tumbled over, screaming. When he rolled over and up again, there was something wrong with his jaw. As he swung his head, the jaw swung too, all bloodied and loose like it was about to come off. The man's eyes were wild, and a sound came out of him I didn't think a man could make. I stood frozen in place, still holding that stupid branch in my hands.

Mr. Sturgess grabbed Edward by his shirt and pulled him up. Edward was coughing and sputtering, and had a faraway look in his eyes, but he still tried to give the man a limp kick before Mr. Sturgess flung him back in my direction.

"Back to the house."

He said it without raising his voice, but there was no questioning his authority in that moment, or the consequences that would follow soon enough.

"Yes sir."

I started going back right then and there, but Edward stayed back to watch as Mr. Sturgess approached the kneeling man, the hatchet moving back and forth between his hands. I tugged on Edward's shirt, wanting to get away from there more than anything. My brother absently wiped at the blood on his face and didn't even seem to notice me.

Finally, Edward let me pull him along. As we went, I heard a grunt, then a sound I'd never want to hear again, the wet thunk of that hatchet meeting flesh. We didn't hear anything more after that. We went back to the house, washed up, and waited for our punishment.

When Mr. Sturgess came back into the house, his hands were bloody and his sleeves covered in dirt. We knew he'd killed and buried the man, just as we knew he'd never speak a word of it to us. We expected a beating, but it didn't come. He cleaned his hands for a long time, took the tea that Mrs. Sturgess gave him, then went into his study and closed the door.

"To bed," Mrs. Sturgess said.

Later, in our cramped bedroom upstairs, we both lay awake staring at the rafters. It was so cold we could see our breath. Edward moaned from the pain in his head. It was bad enough that he threw up his dinner, but he wouldn't let me ask Mrs. Sturgess about seeing a doctor. My brother just wanted to lie there in the quiet, which we did until he finally spoke.

"You left me, Rand."

"I came back."

THE GUEST CHILDREN

71

"But you left."

"I was about to hit him."

"There was a knife on his belt. You could have grabbed it and stuck him with it."

He said it so casually, as if it was nothing for a twelve-year-old boy to kill a grown man with a knife. I didn't want him to be angry at me. I'd come back, after all. And I was going to do something, truly I was. But something changed in my brother after that day, something got broken and didn't mend right, and things between us were never the same.

As time passed, I watched Edward's moods become more volatile. He'd go from quiet and content to a bug-eyed rage or jittering paranoia without any warning at all. There was nothing I could do, except try to keep him out of trouble. I largely failed to manage that, but I tried. The guilt I felt over running away that time in the woods would keep me by Edward's side for the rest of our lives. It kept me back from the war. I'd wanted to serve my country, but instead I fought to keep my younger brother alive and out of jail.

But I didn't complain about it to him. Rarely did I even gripe to myself about my lot in life. Because when I wasn't minding Edward, I had nothing to occupy my thoughts but my own darkness. I could never shake the sight of him, choked and helpless, when I came back to find him by the shack. Or of that man on his knees in the woods with those bright-blue eyes, the jaw hanging off his face like a loose scarf. And then there were my memories of Mr. Sturgess.

Someone bumped into my seat on the train then, and I woke up in a sweat. I was still in my place, still travelling north. It was all just as it was when I'd gone under. The same smoke and chatter, the rumbling wheels beneath me. But one thing was different now.

That dead drifter was sitting across from me, staring at me with those blue eyes of his, his mutilated mouth yawning open in a red scream.

I flung myself backwards in my seat, and heard a woman cry out in the row behind me. I didn't make a sound, but held my hands curled in front of me, ready to defend myself. There was such a clamour of blood surging through me that I felt lightheaded, but I blinked it off as the dead man kept staring back at me.

Except it wasn't that man at all. This man wore a blue uniform.

He was the same RCAF man I'd seen on the platform. His face was red and scarred but not bloody. He was clean-shaven. But he did have those blue eyes, fixed on me so fiercely I felt like they were pinning me to the seatback. There was a florid man in a dusty suit sitting next to the RCAF man. He looked from my cocked fists to the airman's impassive face in front of them.

"What do you think you're doing, son?"

I lowered my hands.

"You should show him some respect," he said.

The airman still stared. I didn't know if he was fixing to

THE GUEST CHILDREN

hit me or just to keep eyeing me until one of us finally gave up our seat.

A few more passengers chimed in then, a story growing that I'd mocked the man for the way he looked and had threatened to clobber him if he didn't change seats. The story spread so quickly and with such certainty that within a minute most of the train was muttering their ill will towards me, with a few passengers outright shouting for me to leave the car. When it was suggested that I be tossed off the train, I got up to move. A few shoulders bounced off me as I went, but I kept moving on a straight path.

I looked back once before I left the car. The man in blue just sat there, completely unaffected. I could see now that he'd not been staring at me at all. He kept gazing into the seat I'd just occupied, even though I was no longer in it. His body was rigid under his uniform, his scarred head held high. As I moved into the next car, I wondered how his nightmares would stack up to mine. I guessed I wouldn't care to trade.

★ ★ ★

Chapter 14

When I climbed off the train in Coal River, I learned there was no easy way to Creekmont. There was a bus that went, sometimes but not always, and anyway, I'd missed it today. My best bet was to wait at the service station and try to talk someone into a ride.

While I was leaving the station, I saw three children waiting outside—two girls and a boy. Their clothes were ill-fitting, all too small for them, and they each had a piece of luggage with a number on it. One of them, the lone boy and the youngest of the three, carried a gas mask over one shoulder. I didn't see a chaperone around, but when I heard them speaking, I caught their English accents and decided it was worth trying to talk to them.

"Hello," I said.

"Good day," the elder girl said. She looked down at her shoes instead of at me.

"Where might you be travelling with those big cases?"

"Home to London and our mum and dad."

THE GUEST CHILDREN

"Oh, that's nice. Have you been here a very long time?"

"Since forever," she said.

"We're the last ones," the younger of the two girls said. "We've been living with Mr. and Mrs. Riley. They were nice. But I didn't care for the school."

"Did you meet any other children from London? I'm looking for a boy and girl named Michael and Frances, last name Hawksby."

"We didn't meet anyone but Canadians," the boy said.

"You didn't hear of other children from London staying around here?"

They hadn't, and they didn't want to talk to me anymore, so I left them there and walked down the road to the service station. I had to ask a few different drivers before I found one who'd let me hitch a ride to Creekmont. He was a deathly quiet man with a twitchy moustache. He smoked and took my coins for fuel with yellowed fingers, examining them closely before slipping them in the lapel pocket of a green corduroy jacket.

It was a long ride, made worse when the rain hit, but after an hour and a half I climbed, stiff-limbed, out of the man's car. Creekmont was a small lakeside town with just one bit of paved road. The main street didn't have but ten storefronts on it. There was a small marina at the end of the road, but hardly anyone was about that afternoon. I caught a sour, rotten-egg smell in the air, which I imagined was coming from the pulp mill I could see through the fog down the lake. I noticed a handbill in a shop window, a church meeting to honour the town's dead at the end of the war. The list of names was longer than I would have imagined for a place so small.

I found a general store that also served as Creekmont's postal station and telegram office. Inside, the shelves were ill-stocked, and the only other customer was a woman looking at a magazine. There was a painted soldier on the cover, entering a house with one bag slung over his shoulder, the straps of two others crossing his chest. *They Are Returning.*

At the counter, I found a young woman in glasses, wearing a plaid dress that looked homemade. She peered up at me as she refilled a penny candy jar. I talked about the recent rain, asked about the town, and then told her I was looking for some children by the name of Hawksby, Guest Children from London who'd stayed in the area during the war.

She scrunched up her face at that. "Well, I certainly think I would have heard about something like that around here."

"But you haven't."

"I'm afraid not. Are they relatives of yours? You don't sound English."

"I don't. But I am. I've been here since I was a boy. And these children, yes, they're distant relatives of mine. They were meant to be sent back home to England by now, but we've had no word, so I've come up to see if I can find them."

THE GUEST CHILDREN

77

"Oh no." She stopped what she was doing then, a last piece of candy clattering into the jar. "I hope they're all right."

"Do you know of a place called Blank Lake?"

"I haven't been there, but I know the name from the maps we sell. I've just about memorized them all by now." She took one of the printed maps from a carousel and spread it out on the counter. "Blank Lake is further north from us here. It's just a tiny little one, see? I believe you can only get there by boat. Peculiar name for a lake, don't you think?"

"It is, yes."

"Whoever first bought that land, they were supposed to name it, but on the deed, they left it blank. So it just became Blank Lake. At least, that's what I was told. Like I said, I've never been there. I don't know anyone who has, to tell you the truth."

"Is there some kind of a resort or a hotel on the lake?"

"I think it closed some years ago. Before the war. I've heard some people still live there, but they don't come into town. Maybe they go to Bristow for their supplies."

"How can I get there?"

"You'd be best off going over to the Shreve Harbour Marina on Lake Carver. It's not too far. We've got one taxi here who'll take you. There's a little stand down the street thataway, with a sign. You can sit there and wait until the car's free."

"And I can catch a boat from the marina?"

"If Mr. Schust will take you. He runs the marina there.

Kind of a funny old man." She lowered her voice then. "And a German. You'll have to come to an arrangement with him. His marina isn't on Blank Lake, but he could likely get you there by boat."

I thanked her and told her I thought there should be a wire transfer waiting for me there. She looked through her records, but the funds hadn't arrived. It irked me, but I decided to keep going towards the resort. I'd pick up the money on the way back. If it still wasn't there, I knew where to find the man.

I went out and sat on a bench by the taxi stand to watch the world go by. Not much of anything passed. The smell was worse than before, and I saw a yellowish foam on the shore at the end of the road. When a car pulled up with a little paper Taxi sign in the window, I spoke to the driver and told him where I wanted to go. He waved me into the car, and I sat there waiting while he went to use the restroom and get a coffee. While I waited, I wondered what Edward was doing, until I reminded myself it was probably best not to think about it.

When we arrived at the Shreve Harbour Marina, it was near suppertime. The Closed sign was in the window, but I could see that the lights were on inside. After a couple of knocks a man came to the door, frowning. He had a long white beard, stained rust-orange with juice from the tobacco he chewed. He wore a work shirt and suspenders holding up denim trousers.

"Closed," he said.

THE GUEST CHILDREN   79

"I see that. I'm wondering if you can help me anyway."

"Closed means closed."

"I've got money . . ."

"Hmm."

I took that as an invitation to continue, so I did. "You're Mr. Schust, aren't you? I need to get to the resort on Blank Lake. Tonight, if I can. I heard you might be able to get me there."

"No." The man turned and was about to close the door in my face.

"Hold on, please. I'm looking for two children from London. Frances and Michael Hawksby. Do you know them?" He didn't answer, so I carried on. "It's an urgent matter, you see. A family matter. And like I said, I have money."

Mr. Schust stood there holding the door, his back to me. "I don't know of these children, and I don't go to Blank Lake anymore. Can't."

Now that he'd strung a few words together, I noticed the German accent the shopgirl mentioned. "What do you mean, you *can't*?"

"The channel that leads between this lake, which is Lake Carver, and that one . . . it's too shallow now to pass through right now. Been a dry summer up until this week. Can't pass until we get some more rain."

"Surely there must be a way to get there, or for the people who live there to get *here*?"

"Couldn't tell you." He turned back to me. "The place

you're looking for is Glass Point Lodge. There is a road, but . . ."

"I was told there's no road leading there."

"There isn't. Not directly. But there's a path. I can drop you at the trailhead, a two-or three-hour hike for you from the closest spot on the road. It'll cost you two dollars. You don't have too much to carry, so you should be able to manage, if it's so important to you."

"You really haven't heard of any children staying over there?"

"I haven't heard anything from those people in some time."

I had doubts about finding my way through the woods, and starting so late in the day, but there looked to be no other choice. The thought of waiting for a fresh start the next day was disagreeable, so I told him yes—even at what he was charging, which would bring me close to the end of my own funds. I couldn't leave Edward alone for too long.

The old man took the suitcase from my hand. He carried it to a rusted truck parked near the docks. The marina was empty. It didn't look like it did much business at the best of times. Climbing into the truck, I watched Schust spit his tobacco onto the sandy lot, wipe his hands, and climb behind the wheel. We started along one dirt road, then another. It was slow going, even in the truck, as the road was potholed and damp from the rain. Always, on either side of us was either a wall of trees or a face of sheer rock, each as imposing as the other.

"You know anything about the people who live out here on Blank Lake?"

"No."

"I used to live on a farm a little further north from here. As I recall, we knew who most of our neighbours were back then, or at least what they did for a trade."

He scoffed at that by way of an answer.

"It's some kind of an inn or a resort out there, I'm told?"

"Was. It closed."

"Why?"

"Couldn't say."

"Do you know the name of the owners?"

Schust gave me a sharp look to let me know there was no point in asking more questions. I looked out the window and saw a rundown cabin by the woodside, green moss growing up its walls and over its sagging roof. We drove on in silence for a time, until we turned onto yet another dirt track with more towering trees on either side. Even in daylight, I couldn't see much beyond a few feet into the woods. After a few minutes, Schust stopped the truck, the brakes moaning as it shuddered to a standstill.

"The trail's not been used in a while, so keep your eyes sharp, yes? It's nearly five o'clock now. You've got a few good hours of light left. Don't dawdle. The lake is straight east from the road. As long as you find the water, you'll be all right. Once you start walking in circles, you might never find your way again. Over there's Crown land. Over there, too. Nobody else lives around here."

"Understood."

Schust climbed out with me and rummaged in the back of the truck. He pulled at some nautical rope in a loose, wet pile and cut off two lengths of it for me.

"Some straps should make that case easier to carry."

"Appreciate it. I might ring you when I'm done out there, to see if I can catch a ride back from here with you."

"There won't be a telephone. If you can get them to take you back to the end of Blank Lake and cross the strip of land there, you'll come to Lake Carver and a stone cottage. The family that lives there, by the name of Terrace, they can take you to the marina and I'll help you get back to where you need to go."

I thanked Schust. He nodded, then took another plug of tobacco from a pouch and put it in his mouth, breathing through his nose while he started to chew. It seemed like he was going to say something else, but he examined me for a moment before he did.

"You back from the war?" he asked.

"No sir. I've been working as a builder."

"Things always need building."

"Indeed, they do."

Schust nodded again and then climbed into the truck. I stood by the side of the road, watching him drive away. The truck disappeared around a bend. Only then did it hit me just how stranded I was. It was a cool day for August, the wind nudging the trees hard enough that they heaved

The Guest Children

and waved on either side of the road. It felt like a welcome, or a warning.

I thought about walking back the way we'd come, going to shelter in that derelict cabin until the next morning, but it seemed like the worse of the two ways to go. At least, if I made it to the lodge, there'd be food and a bed, and maybe some answers about the children.

Eyeing the trailhead, little more than a sliver of gap in the tight-packed tree line, I figured the walk would be the fastest route to get me back to Edward, even as it took me farther from him. I knew my brother so well that I could almost see him there in the apartment, peering out the peephole, watching for my return. If all went well, I'd be back in two days, maybe three. Any longer than that, I might not like what I found when I got home.

★ ★ ★

CHAPTER 15

Taking the lengths of lake-damp rope Schust gave me, I tied cow hitches around the handle of my suitcase to make straps I could sling over my shoulders. When we were boys, Edward taught me all the knots I knew. He had an old book of them on the Sturgess farm, and he practised and practised, crazy about all the things he could do with a piece of old rope.

Edward was like that. When something caught his fancy, he'd dive into it headfirst. Wouldn't come up for air until he'd worn it out. He was like that with liquor too, even at twelve, before we fled from the farm. That was the real start of the rough times. I didn't like my brother when he was drunk—not then, and even less so when we moved to the city. In those days, Edward turned mean when his switch flipped, and it flipped more often than not. I stuck with him, tried to keep him from hurting anyone or taking too bad a beating over his foul temper. Sometimes I took a punch, but most of the time it stopped him from taking

THE GUEST CHILDREN   85

twenty. Usually, the men my brother went after just wanted to save face and get the hell away from him.

I didn't blame them. A lot of the time, I wanted the same thing.

When we were still living with the Sturgess family, Edward discovered he could steal from our neighbour's still. Drink became the whole focus of his world. If Mr. Sturgess had ever smelled it on him or seen him drunk, he'd have beaten him half to death. But I kept him from that.

I tried to water down the booze when Edward wasn't looking, to protect him from getting caught. The drink made him mouthy and belligerent, and Mr. Sturgess would not let such trespasses go without putting someone in their place. Adding water to my brother's purloined liquor jars was the best and only plan I had. It worked for a while, but not for long. When Edward finally figured out what I was doing, he went quiet for a few days. He wouldn't look at me or speak to me, and for the first time I found myself afraid of my own younger brother.

One night I woke up in our room. He'd disappeared somewhere. After watering down his jar again, I must've been in a deep sleep. That, or Edward knew how to move me so gently that I didn't wake. As I slept, he'd taken some dusty old length of farm rope and tied me up a dozen ways to my cot, without me ever opening my eyes. The knots were so tight I could hardly draw breath, especially when I started to panic. I pushed and I strained in the middle of the night, trying not to wake Mr. Sturgess. Eventually I flipped the cot on its side with my exertions. But I never could get free of those knots. Edward wanted to show what he could do.

When my brother came back, hours later, he was staggering. I heard Mrs. Sturgess downstairs in the kitchen, but he must've slipped past her somehow. Edward had that grim look on his face from drinking when he crept back into our room. But when he saw me there on the cold floor, all trussed up like I was fixing to get slaughtered, the look dropped away. I saw my brother come back. He wept quietly as he untied me and then he poured the rest of his bottle out the window and said he was done with it. And he was, for a while.

I was thinking about that night, hiking through the woods with the rope straps I'd made for my suitcase biting through my jacket into my shoulders. The trail was already choking with overgrowth here, and the canopy overhead thick enough to sieve out most of the light from the sun, but there was still a faint sense of a passage ahead. After a few more paces I noticed a black spot on one of the tree trunks. It was a relief to see it there. If the trail was marked with those spots all the way to the resort, I'd have no problem getting there before nightfall. The journey might not be quite as bad as I'd come to fear.

Still, there was something disquieting about those woods. They were stifling with overgrowth. Not in the kind of lush green I remembered from the forests of my childhood.

THE GUEST CHILDREN   87

This green was pallid, a suffocating and sickly yellowish blur all around. I walked for an hour, probably more, with thirst creeping up on me. It was stupid of me not to ask Schust for a flask or some food. I kept thinking I heard a creek nearby, but I couldn't find the source of the sound. But in the few minutes I spent veering off the trail to look for it, I noticed something else.

Those black spots, the ones I'd guessed were trail markers, were now on every single tree I passed. Spots from some disease, maybe, not markers.

I thought I'd barely stepped off the trail at the sound of water, but already I'd lost any sight of my path. The veiled sun was lower now, shadowed tree limbs interlacing across the forest floor. I spun in circles, taking my arms out of the suitcase straps to rest my sore shoulders. There were spots of red on my shirt where the rope had rubbed the skin raw even in the short time since I'd set out on foot. I listened and peered through the trees, hoping to see a glint of lake water to lead me to shore, where I could get the lay of the land and a drink, but a steady breeze was rustling the branches and I couldn't hear anything over the sound of it.

I carried on again, the suitcase now hanging from one tired arm. My toes and heels screamed from blisters in my city shoes, but I kept slogging in the direction I thought was forward, slipping on damp roots and rocks. The earth seemed to have been scraped away in places, leaving behind sheets of stone with dark fissures deep and wide enough to swallow a leg.

After I passed through a dense stand of birch and undergrowth, I came to a clearing. There was a shack standing there. The clearing was small, not much bigger than the room I shared with Edward. As for the structure, it looked very much like the shack we'd built in the woods back when we lived on the farm, the one we tried to replicate in the valley as grown men. Maybe a little better built than ours, and with a stovepipe sticking out the side, but I supposed all shacks look more or less the same.

I called out, "Hello . . . ?"

The shack shook slightly, like someone had moved inside.

The sight of it shook me too. I stepped back. I called out again, but no one answered or came out. All I could hear now was the tree canopy whispering overhead. I took a step closer to the shack, and then another. Most likely it was just some animal nesting inside. I wondered, unsettled, if I'd need to shelter in this place overnight and set out again at dawn.

Drawing closer to the shack's entrance, I saw a dirty bedsheet hanging over the opening. I stood before it, feeling foolish in my hesitation.

"Hello?"

No one answered, but as I reached out my hand to pull the fabric aside and peer into the shadowy space behind it, the shack shook once more. I took another quick step back but felt foolish then, so I darted forward to tug the sheet away from the door. As the tattered fabric fluttered to the ground, I looked inside.

Even with the daylight coming through the opening, it was hard to see much. It was a small space, barely high enough to stand in, no more than six feet by eight in size. I could see all manner of clutter and stepped into the opening for a better look. No sign of whatever animal was living in there, but it couldn't have been anything too big. I stepped inside, down in a crouch under the angled wood stove pipe, and let my eyes adjust to the darkness.

There were piles of junk strewn about. Rotted old books, framed photos marred by mould, and some tarnished trinkets—necklaces, bracelets, brooches, and the like. There was a silver Great War medal, the ribbon rotted and frayed, and the inscribed name worn down to illegibility. The belongings of whoever once stayed here, I guessed. The shack brought back bad memories of our bleak times in the valley, and fresh worries about the harsh and hopeless days Edward and I could be facing again soon.

By then, I'd made up my mind that I wouldn't spend the night here. I didn't like the smell or the feeling of the cramped shack and wanted to get moving again. This slow, nonsensical dread kept creeping over me, a fear that I'd be found lying next to my rotting suitcase, weeds and vines clutching my bones, coaxing them down into the soil to make me part of the forest.

The dark was coming on now, but I hoped that if I

hurried my pace and kept moving in the right direction, I could still find the resort in time. Even if night fell, if I'd got close enough, I might see the lights and let them guide me there. Ducking back through the doorway, I went to set forth again and find the trail I'd lost some way back.

But when I came out of the shack, I was someplace else.

I was in a forest still, but a different one. Right away I recognized it as the woods that bordered on the Sturgess property, where Edward and I built our shack and hid ourselves away from the farm. I knew exactly where I was the moment I saw it. But that wasn't the strangest thing. The strangest thing was that Edward was standing in front of me.

My brother appeared to be ten or eleven years old. He grinned, and then he ran off and disappeared into the trees. I looked down, realizing then that I too was a boy. I recognized the worn leather shoes, the short trousers that Mrs. Sturgess had mended dozens of times, and the shirt with mismatched buttons I was mocked for at school.

"Randall!"

Edward's voice sounded urgent, frightened, and by instinct I hurried to follow him. My movements felt strange, this younger version of my body so small and weak and yet somehow also invincible.

"Where are you?"

"You gotta see this, Rand! It's fantastic!"

That was a word I don't think I'd ever heard my brother

THE GUEST CHILDREN

91

say in his entire life, but I was driven to find him, to see what he was talking about. I kept following his voice, as the woods became darker and less familiar, until I heard the lapping of lake water nearby. As I pushed through the dense trees, the branches scraped jagged red lines into my skin, but I felt no pain.

When I found Edward, he was standing on a narrow strip of beach overlooking a dark lake, a lake that seemed to go on forever. At the horizon, the bruisy twilight sky and the fog-cloaked water seemed to blend into one, such that there was no horizon at all.

"I don't understand," I said. "There was never any lake here before."

He shrugged. "Let's walk to the other side."

"That's not possible, Edward."

"Yes, it is. Come with me."

Edward took a step off the beach and his feet stayed on the surface of the water.

"See? I told you."

He started walking out across the lake, always the reckless one, always the braver of us when we were young. I followed, just a step at first. Somehow, I too stayed on the surface as I walked, hearing small splashes as I put my feet down, but not feeling any damp coming into my shoes at all. Edward skipped ahead, laughing. I tried to catch up to him, but he was too fast.

When my brother disappeared into the fog, I got scared

and started calling out his name. He didn't answer. The sound of his splashing footfalls faded away. I only took one more step before the lake wouldn't hold me up anymore, and the water gave way beneath my feet.

★   ★   ★

CHAPTER 16

I woke up standing in water. When I looked down, I saw that I wasn't in the woods near the shack anymore. Nor was I in that imagined place I'd just visited with young Edward. I was somewhere else entirely, standing knee-deep in the water of a sandy inlet. It was a lake, but not the one I'd just seen. There were tall, imposing slopes of rock rising on either side, with trees at the top blocking out the last of the sunlight.

I had no memory of getting to this place. Turning to look behind me, I saw my shoes and socks neatly placed on the narrow beach. They were next to my suitcase, which was open, its contents scattered across the sand. My footprints traced a meandering path around it, as if I'd been searching for something. At the other side of the strip of beach, my trail originated at the base of a set of wooden stairs leading up the steep face of dark rock.

There was a structure on the sand near the shoreline. Not on it but above it, I saw then. It was in the shape of a grand home, but built on a smaller scale, like a playhouse for children. Standing on log piles, it rose just a few feet above the beach below. I could see an engraving on the side, but I couldn't make out what it said. The window openings had fluttering burlap in them, like curtains. What was inside the structure was too dark to see.

I couldn't imagine how I'd ended up here, with no memory of how I'd travelled. The water was a rich, black-coffee colour, making it hard to see below the surface. Beyond the end of the inlet, I could see the open water of what I assumed must be Blank Lake, and the trees lining the far shore. For a moment I thought I saw a sliver of dock in the distance.

I was deathly cold despite the summer weather, and I wondered how long I'd been standing there. The loss of time and place frightened me, and that only added to the shivering. I needed to get back to shore and find the lodge before it got dark. It was almost dark already, the little remaining light blue-tinged and weakening by the moment.

As I turned around to go back towards the beach, I saw a woman's face under the water.

She was just below the surface, a few feet away from where I stood, and she was looking up at me. Her skin had a yellow pallor in that inky lake, topped by a crown of red hair that swayed slowly from the top of her head. Her dark eyes were open and staring, her features expressionless. I couldn't see anything else of her. She seemed to be wearing some formless black shift that blended into the dark water.

The Guest Children

The sight of her frightened me so much that I shouted, falling backwards into the lake. For a moment, flailing in the shallows, I felt as though a hundred hands were grabbing at me, holding me down under the surface, but nothing stopped me as I thrust myself upright and scrambled to the shore. Soaked and shivering, with my heart thudding a riot and my breath faltering from the water I'd swallowed, I scuttled backwards in the sand, watching the lake for any further sign of her. I could no longer see where she was, which was worse somehow than when I could. Jerking my head to the left and right, I half expected to find her standing over me now, pale hands reaching out as water pattered off her onto the sand.

I scanned the ridge of stone surrounding the inlet, shadows in the trees half forming into new nightmares before I could cast them aside as tricks of the light. My gaze went to the decaying playhouse, and then back to the lake. I waited for the woman to rise, to break the surface and stride through the shallows towards me. She didn't. Nothing stirred the water but a faint breeze. Finally, I convinced myself that the woman was just a cast-off vision, a wayward thread of the strange daydream that brought me to the beach. That's all she could be. No one could hold their breath so long. But even so, I wanted to get out of there.

I stuffed my things back into my suitcase, teeth clacking together in my wet clothes, and then snapped it shut again. Keeping an eye on the lake, I stuck my feet in my shoes and my socks in my pockets. Although I was still dripping wet, I wanted to get going before I changed into something dry.

Moving to the base of the stairs, I considered taking a closer look at the playhouse. A short wooden ladder led up to the platform. I kept expecting to see a face in the window. It would be easy enough to peer inside, but I didn't want to waste any more daylight. I looked at the long stairway climbing the stone face, turning back on itself twice on the way up. It looked neither sturdy nor easy to climb, but I started up the steps and went as quickly as I could.

The stair rail was slick with a damp mould. The feeling of it was so distasteful that I climbed without using the rail for balance. The creaking sound the steps made under my weight echoed off the stone boundaries of the inlet, and it sounded very much like screaming. Halfway up, I caught a flash of something white stuffed into the stair rail. Peering closer, I found a damp and ragged piece of paper. It tugged it out of where it was stuck, unfolded it, and read.

Michael and Frances Hawksby were here.

Well then. I knew that I should be grateful for this sign, but it felt more like a warning than a lucky break. I stuffed the paper in my pocket and kept moving up the steps. I came upon something like a trail again near the top of the stairs, and a sign with an arrow reading *Glass Point Lodge*. It was fully dark now, under a starless and moonless sky, and I moved slowly, hands out in front of me as I did what I

THE GUEST CHILDREN

could to follow the trail. I was still close to the water, which Schust said was a good thing. So long as I kept the water to my left and didn't tumble over the edge and down the rocks, I should be okay.

But I was still cold, and I was frightened too. It took everything I had to shut out the clamouring questions in my mind, like how it was that I'd lost consciousness and moved from one place to another without any memory of it. I kept seeing that woman's face looking up at me, her eyes the colour of peeled green grapes.

For a moment I thought I'd lost the trail again in my distraction. I rummaged in my suitcase for a matchbook. When I found one, mercifully dry, I shielded my eyes from the flare as I lit it, and then used the faint light to make sure I was still on the trail. There was a black spot on the tree next to me, but I knew now that those wouldn't help me.

After the match burned down to my fingers, I cursed and let my eyes readjust before I started walking again. In those first moments of partial blindness, I was sure I saw a figure standing on a high tree branch just down the path, watching me from a height. It was impossible for someone to be so high and stand so still on a branch like that, but I was sure I saw them there. Male or female, I couldn't be sure, but I took a step back at the sight.

As my vision returned to normal, the figure faded away into nothing. The smell of the smoke from my match was surprisingly powerful in the forest. It was only as I hurried along that I realized it wasn't the match at all. It was chimney smoke. And there was a faint yellow light coming through the trees ahead. I thought I heard voices speaking but couldn't make them out.

"Hello!" I called out, my dry tongue barely forming the word.

I kept taking cautious steps forward, pausing to shout for help as I went, hearing the sharp strain of distress in my own voice. Before long, I heard voices answering me in the distance, and saw shadows dancing through the trees in the play of an approaching light.

A woman's voice called back, "Is someone there?"

"Yes! I'm here!"

My voice sounded so small, so boyish, that I had to look down to be sure I was still awake, and still a grown man— not in the grip of another warped dream of my childhood. I heard footsteps and saw two lights bobbing towards me from the other direction, in the grip of shadowy figures I couldn't yet make out. Flying insects, barely noticeable before now, became impossibly loud as they buzzed around my ears and eyes.

When the two figures finally reached me, a woman's pale face peered at me over her lantern. The light was so bright that I had to shield my eyes from it. There was a dark figure behind the woman who I could tell was a man, but he said nothing.

"Who are you?" the woman said. "How did you get here?"

She had an English accent, and long, ashy hair framing

THE GUEST CHILDREN 99

her face, with fine features and eyebrows so pale that at first I thought she had none.

"From the road, I . . ."

I tried to finish answering her, but despite a thundering relief at my rescue, I couldn't form the words. I saw the woman glance back at the big man behind her and caught a glimpse of his bearded face and glittering brown eyes.

"Look at him," the man said. "He's half mad."

She turned back to me then. "Let's get you back to the lodge."

They set off back in the other direction, barely waiting for me to follow. I took a few steps behind them, already afraid they'd leave me behind. That was as far as I got before the weight of my case became so unbearable that I let it drop to the ground. When my body got heavy too, I let it do the same. The ground rushed up to meet me, but I felt nothing when I landed. Lying on the forest floor, I looked up at the orange lamplight playing against the tree canopy overhead. It was like some wilderness cathedral, sacred and secret, and the sight humbled me. I half expected to hear a pipe organ shuddering though the tree trunks. Instead, I heard my rescuers coming back. I tried to rise, but the effort snuffed out whatever I had left in me, and I closed my eyes instead.

★ ★ ★

PART 3

GLASS POINT LODGE

CHAPTER 17

I woke up holding my breath, pain everywhere. I was on my feet in some dim, stuffy room, and I was pointing at the window. Towards what, I didn't know. The curtains were drawn, but I could see cool daylight filtering through the thin fabric. I needed to take in air, but something prevented me from getting it, as if my mouth was seized in the grip of a clammy hand.

Finally, the paralysis broke, and I drew in a long, desperate breath. Panting in the middle of the room, I looked down and saw I'd been stripped to my shorts. The rest of my clothes were dried and folded on a chair, atop my suitcase. My rope-burned shoulders were dressed in bandages. My feet were bandaged too. There was a glass of water on the wicker table next to one of the two sagging beds, the one with tangled sheets and the vague outline of my body. I picked up the water and drained it in one gulp, feeling grit in my mouth as I swallowed.

My stomach, empty since lunch the day before, shot

pains through me in protest. I looked around as the cramps subsided. It had the drab, anonymous look of a rented room, one that hadn't seen a guest in a long time. There were water stains on the ceiling, the wallpaper was peeling in places, and a musty-closet smell pervaded everything. The faded portrait of the King hanging over the bed was the wrong George by nearly a decade. I went to the window, parted the curtains, and looked out in the direction I'd been pointing in my sleep. I could see a boathouse, a dock, and the lake beyond.

Gripping the window frame, I tried to piece things together. Before I could even remember how I'd ended up in the room, the grim details of the nightmare I'd just escaped came creeping back up on me. I'd gone to that same imagined beach of all my dreams, in the aftermath of battle. It started with me knee-deep in sea water, waves surging at the backs of my legs. It was night. Around me, there were craters in the sand under slithering billows of smoke, and the still bodies of many dead. Once more, I was looking for someone.

Wading towards shore, it was hard for me to make out more than the vague shapes of ruined buildings and shattered trees beyond the beach. From time to time, a foot or head would brush against me in the water, and I'd recoil as I pushed the dead man away. I called out once to see if anyone could hear me, but I stopped when I didn't like the way my voice echoed in the silence. When I reached the water's edge, there was a new sound. A kind of hollow, sucking sound—a drainpipe's hiss, or the thirsty void of an empty tin can next to your ear. I felt the sound vibrating in the water and juddering through my stomach.

I saw the soldier then. He was just ahead of me, near a tangled spool of barbed wire. His face was turned up towards the tree canopy, his back arched in agony, but he was as still as a statue. He was floating two feet above the ground. Something spooled out of holes in his chest and belly, mixing in the night air. It looked like sand, coming out of him slowly, like cream drizzled into black coffee.

The sight was both so real and so strange that I only watched, until I heard a rush of wind coming through the trees towards me. When the wind hit the soldier, he collapsed into grains of sand that fell back onto the beach with the sound like trilling the high keys of an out-of-tune piano. The sand blew straight into my eyes, blinding me. I staggered, trying to rub my vision clear, but the sand ground into my eyeballs.

When I could see again, the soldier was in front of me. He pointed at me with a milk-pale hand. His face was already disappearing, the features melting off him grain by grain and leaving a blank oval of sand. I felt in some cold and slithering part of me that the blankness was smiling.

That was when I woke, on my feet and with my own finger outstretched, in what could only be a guest room at Glass Point Lodge. At the window now, I remembered my encounter with the two people in the woods, a sense of movement after my fall, and the vague murmurs of strangers' voices. Beyond that, there was only the dream. Another in a long line of dreams about a war fought without me. In the night, my guilt took me there.

But it was morning now, and I had some things to work out. There was something under my bare feet, a fine layer of sand blanketing the floor. That was not so strange, since the room wasn't clean. But the sand was perfectly dispersed, like the fine dusting of icing sugar Mrs. Sturgess sifted over her boiled raisin cake. I saw my footprints through it, leading from the tousled bed where I'd been sleeping to the window. There was another set of footprints, smaller ones, that led through the sand and stopped right before the bed. The footprints approached, but I couldn't see any going back the other way, as if whoever left them had then vanished when they'd found me.

There was something else in the room that caught my eye. The silver war medal I'd found in the shack, with the frayed and rotted ribbon. It sat atop my clothing now. I must've pocketed it without meaning to, but I was certain I'd left it behind.

Gingerly, feeling new pains speaking up throughout my body, I put on my clothes. I shook the sand off my bare feet before I put on my socks, then upended my shoes to get some out of them as well. The sound it made when it fell brought back the dream again. I picked some of it up in my fingers. When I shook it off, it made that same faint, atonally musical sound I'd heard in the dream, a faraway wind chime made from mismatched bells.

THE GUEST CHILDREN 107

Crossing the floor, I went to the door to turn the cracked glass knob. The floorboards creaked under me, and the door stuck for a moment. In that breathless second, I thought I'd been locked in, but it was only swelled in the frame and pulled free with a little effort.

When it did, there was a woman standing there on the other side, smiling at me—the same woman I'd encountered in the forest the night before. I had the strangest impression that she'd just been hovering there with that forced grin and stiff pose, waiting for me to emerge.

"Mr. Sturgess," she said. "Welcome to Glass Point Lodge."

I was caught off guard finding her there, both by her strange affect and by the fact that she so readily knew my name.

"We looked at your identification," she said.

"Oh, of course."

"We met last night in the woods . . . do you remember that?"

"I do. I owe you my thanks, and my apologies for the state I was in—"

"Never mind that. My name is Theresa Mast. I own the lodge with my husband, Simon. We're just happy that you're all right. You *are* all right, aren't you?"

"I think so. Thank you for taking me in. I didn't have an easy time getting here."

"Nobody's used that trail in ages. We were astonished you made it as far as you did."

"Surely people must come and go from here somehow?"

"There's a man at the end of the lake who brings us supplies as we need them. We haven't felt much reason to leave recently. With the war on, of course. This is our refuge." She smiled again then. "I'm curious what brought you here, considering we're so out of the way, and we haven't advertised for guests in years."

I opened my mouth to answer, but before I could, Theresa grabbed my hand and pulled me out of the room. Releasing me as we started down the hall, she waved for me to follow her along to a narrow spiral staircase.

"If you come down now to meet the others, you won't have to tell it twice."

We went down the creaky steps, into a vaulted reception area with great wood beams meeting at the highest point. Dust motes and cobwebs floated in dull morning light. The front desk, crafted of half-cut logs with a solid plank top, was piled with junk—old newspapers, cleaning supplies, books, and mismatched china.

"Mind the mess," she said.

"Where are we going, Mrs. Mast?"

"The dining room. Please call me Theresa." She looked back at me with that unnerving smile. "You must be hungry."

As we passed through the lobby, we turned into the dining room. Here, too, there were dusty wood timbers overhead and walls hewn of grey stone. Three large windows

The Guest Children

109

looked out upon a formidable wall of dark forest, the sight of which made me a little uneasy. The lodge reminded me of the Sturgess place, but built on a much grander scale. Despite the big windows, the room was dim. There were a dozen or so round tables placed about. Most had no chairs.

Seated in the room were four people of varying ages. There was a large, thick-bearded man in middle age—the man I'd seen in the woods the night before—alone at one table with a pipe, a cup of coffee or tea, and an open book in front of him. There was a stooped, thin, and balding older man in Great War service dress, missing a hand. Seated across from him was a slightly younger woman in a dressing gown, her white hair up in a bun. And lastly, a dark-haired woman about my age in a tidy grey dress, who sat alone and was staring at me.

"Everyone," Theresa said. "This is Mr. Randall Sturgess. He's come to us all the way from Toronto. Thankfully, he seems no worse for wear after his difficult journey."

"Hello," I said.

"You came in from the road on foot, we hear . . ." the military man said. "And got yourself a little turned around."

"I had business here, and it seemed the only way . . . I was told the channel from Lake Carver was not passable by boat."

There was a scattering of yesses and hmms, and then more of the quiet. A moth trapped inside the room bashed against the window twice before retreating to the ceiling to hover near another outdated portrait of the King. I think they all expected me to speak, but I was unsure what to say next. This much I knew: I saw no children and heard no children.

Theresa soon broke the silence. "I'm sure you could do with a cup of tea. And I'll go see about some breakfast as well."

"Thank you."

"Back in a moment."

Theresa left the room then and I stood awkwardly by the door as they all stared at me.

"I'm Simon Mast," the man with the beard said. "Theresa is my wife. This is our lodge. And here," he said, pointing to the older man and woman as they put on wide smiles, "is Mr. Julian Farthing and Miss Agatha Jansons."

Agatha said, "Julian's a widower and I'm a spinster. But rest assured there's nothing scandalous going on between us."

"Pleased to know you, Randall," Julian said. "It's been some time since we've seen a new face around here. We'll be eager to hear news from the world."

"Well, I'm sure you've had the good news that the war is over."

Agatha laughed then, a throaty laugh that turned into a rumbling cough. She lit a cigarette and waved the smoke from her face. Simon watched her, disapprovingly I thought, and then turned back to me.

Simon tugged at his beard. "Is it really, after all this time?"

"You hadn't heard?"

The younger woman seated alone spoke up then. "We've had no news here, for ages now. No papers, no radio. We heard of the German surrender, but not this. I can hardly believe it. There must be such joy in the streets."

"You could say that, yes."

"It helps to know that our sacrifices were not for nothing," she said.

Julian and Agatha looked down at the table. Simon sighed and introduced us. "Randall Sturgess, this is Mrs. Helena Heitmann."

I nodded to her. "I'm pleased to meet you, Mrs. Heitmann."

"Mrs. Heitmann escaped from Austria just before the war," Simon added before she could respond. He blinked as everyone turned to look at him.

Helena cast a blank look in Simon's direction, then turned back to me. "I came to your country with my husband. He went back there to fight, but he didn't return."

"My condolences," I said.

"And you, you've lost someone also, I think. You have that look."

"No, I was one of the fortunate."

"I'm glad to hear it. I look forward to speaking later, Mr. Sturgess. Please excuse me."

"Of course."

As Helena walked out of the room, soft shoes whispering over the linoleum, Julian announced in his hoarse, whispery voice that he was going to take some air. Agatha pulled her gown tighter over her chest, as though she'd just noticed she was still wearing it.

"I believe I'll get dressed," she said.

"Pleasure to meet you both."

Julian grunted in response. Agatha rose, coughed, glanced out the window at the wall of forest, then looked back at me.

"Nice to have a new face," she said.

As Agatha passed by me on her way out, I nodded. I nodded again when Julian left by a different door leading to a screened porch off the dining room. I couldn't help but feel that those gathered had just fled from my presence. Simon indicated the seat next to him and I moved to sit there. He watched my every movement, the way shopkeepers used to watch Edward and me walking their aisles in our grubby clothes. I wondered what Simon thought I was going to steal.

"Safe to say you didn't know what you were getting into when you set out on your journey yesterday," he said. "It was foolish. You're fortunate we found you."

"The man at the marina, Schust . . . he led me to believe it was possible. But I must've got turned around at some point. The trail was overgrown, and the landscape . . ."

"Quite disorienting, yes. And dangerous to traverse with all those narrow slits in the rock, so many roots to trip you up. It's understandable for a man to lose his way."

Theresa came back then with some weak-looking tea, no milk, and toast made with some dry and dense bread. I needed both, but I had to dunk the bread in the tea to

THE GUEST CHILDREN 113

soften it before I dared try to chew. Theresa watched me labouring over the bread as she sat.

"Our supplies are running low. The food here isn't what it used to be."

"It's good. Thank you. And thank you again for coming to my aid last night."

Simon sipped from his cup and I could smell the liquor inside it, which made me think of my brother, who was probably drinking by now himself. We sat there in silence, and I watched Simon use a fingernail to scrape something off the table before I spoke up again.

"You must be wondering why I'm here."

"Indeed yes," Simon said, his voice flat and uncurious.

"I've come looking for your niece and nephew, Michael and Frances Hawksby. On behalf of their father's family in England. I was told they've been living here at the resort. Are they here now?"

Theresa looked sharply at Simon, but he kept his gaze on the interior of his cup. We sat like this for some time, with Theresa staring at her husband and Simon deliberately not looking back, until Theresa rose from the table.

"I was afraid that's why you'd come," she said. "I'll leave Simon to tell you about it. I'm afraid I don't have it in me."

"Love," Simon said. "Don't."

"I'll just go do the washing-up."

I watched Theresa walk out. To tell you about *it,* she'd said. Not *them.*

Simon wiped a hand down his face. "Ah, God," he said. "Goddamn her."

"Aren't the children here?"

"Have you seen any children around?"

"No. But I was told they were living at this lodge. They were meant to spend the war with you, weren't they? And I saw some footprints in my room."

Simon frowned. "No, no. Those must be old. Very old." "Then where are Frances and Michael, Simon?"

"What business is it of yours?"

"I told you, the Hawksby family—"

"We already let everyone in England know what happened. We wrote to them years ago. You've wasted your time travelling here."

"They've had no messages from you at all, which is why I've been hired. If there's some bad news, they haven't received it. So why don't you just tell *me* what happened, Simon."

"Yes, it's bad. It's very bad, all right?" Simon rose, motioning for me to follow without meeting my eye, leaving the chair askew from the table. I didn't move from my seat. He too glanced out the window at the woods before he finally looked at me once more. "Please, let me tell you about it as I take you around the lodge. I've learned that I'm less likely to weep if I'm walking about."

★ ★ ★

Chapter 18

I'd only been a night guard back when I worked for the security agency, but they'd put me with an old-timer at the start, a man named Roy who'd worked there for decades. Roy used to do more detective work in his younger days, and he taught me things—like how to tell when a person might be lying, how to lay out the stories people told you in your head so you could see what didn't fit. Already, I'd seen the signs. The way Simon occupied himself fussing with the table, and how he continued to avoid my eye as we walked out of the dining room. He was using the needless tour to distract me, to delay telling me what had become of the children. But I figured if I played along, I might be able to get more out of him than he meant to let on.

"You may as well get the lay of the land," Simon said. "Although I suppose you won't be here for long."

"Why do you suppose that?"

He carried on into the lobby, even more sad and decrepit

than it seemed upon first impression. Weak rays from an overcast sun strained through grimy windows, casting a pallid glow on what was once an impressive reception area. I could see the faint gleam of Blank Lake beyond the glass, and the shape of the dock and the boathouse I'd spotted from my room.

The cluttered front desk looked like it hadn't checked in a new guest since before the war, which I assumed to be the case. I noted water damage in the ceiling and on the floor, more dust veins swaying in the high corners, and peeled paint on the walls. Spotting some framed photographs of the lodge's more prosperous days, I made a note to look at them later.

"This is the lobby," Simon said.

I followed him through swinging doors off the lobby into a large, white-tiled kitchen. At some point I imagined these facilities were able to feed dozens of guests. Now, the room smelled of old grease and mousetraps that needed clearing out. Some old furniture was piled along one side, vastly reducing the workable space, and the windows were papered over like the ones in our apartment at home. There was hardly anything on the shelves, just a few tins of food and large but near-empty bags of flour and sugar.

"The kitchen," Simon said.

Although Theresa said she'd left us to do the washing-up, I could see the breakfast dishes piled and abandoned in the sink. She was nowhere to be seen. Simon turned to leave, but I stayed rooted where I was, trying to hold his eye and read his countenance. He looked away, first at the floor and then towards the covered window facing the back of the lodge. Simon's face twisted in something most likely meant to present as a sad smile. It looked more like nausea.

"I can see that you're impatient. But it's so bloody painful to talk about. I'm afraid we've gotten into a habit of avoiding the subject. It doesn't change anything, but it makes it easier."

"It is a simple question, Simon—where are Michael and Frances?"

"It's not simple, you see . . . because the truth is, we don't know."

"What do you mean, *you don't know*? Those children were your wards."

"They were here, yes. They came in the autumn of 1940. After they lost their parents in the Blitz, the poor dears. And we took good care of them for a time, truly."

Simon walked out of the room then and through another door. This one led to a compact old ballroom with dusty-rose walls, a raised stage with a painted landscape backdrop that looked more like rural England than northern Ontario, and a cloakroom off to one side. I followed him, the loose parquet flooring shifting and popping under my feet. It was dark with the curtains drawn, but not so dark that I couldn't make out the state of disrepair in the room.

"We used to host grand weddings here, if you can believe that. Everyone came in by boat. We had a cellar full of fine wines, and a marvellous chef."

118   Patrick Tarr

I looked at the outside wall, which had pink wallpaper sloughing off it in mouldering strips. A couple of the windows were cracked or outright broken, and it looked like there was an abandoned wasps' nest tucked into a corner of the ceiling above the stage. There was a quiet stillness in the room's air, and I could hear Simon's breathing in it, the pace of it quicker than it had any reason to be.

"When did you last see the children?"

"It's been years now, I'm afraid."

"And in all that time, you told no one what happened?"

"I didn't say that."

"And yet the Hawskby family has had no news."

"That's no fault of ours. We did everything we could."

Simon shrugged. He was a big man, taller and broader than me, but I still had a rising urge to grab him by his wool shirt and shake the truth out of him. Simon didn't give me the chance, once again walking out of the room before I could ask him another question.

I followed, again, and we crossed back through the lodge, ending up seated at a table in the screened porch. The air was heavy and smelled of the lake. Simon tried to clean some of the grime off this table too, but he gave up under my watchfulness and absently wiped his hands on his trousers. He could see from my face that I'd had enough of his games.

"Well, those children simply ran away and that's the whole truth of it." Simon let out a kind of sad, desperate groan. "They just left us. We looked everywhere, truly we did. But to no avail. I fear that they didn't want to be found, but I can't imagine why."

"How long ago was this?"

"A long time now. Just after they arrived."

"That would have been September of 1940?"

"October or November, I should think."

I took out my little notebook and wrote that down. Simon didn't like me doing that. I could see him staring at the page, trying to read upside down as I wrote. Turning the book, I showed him what I'd written. He stopped looking then.

"How long were they here before they went missing? How long exactly."

"Weeks. Three or four weeks."

I wondered what kind of city children would run off into dense, imposing woods like these after only a few weeks in the area. As far as I could tell, they knew no one else in the country. They likely had no money or any idea of where to go. None would do it, I thought. Not unless there was something they feared even more than the wild landscape looming around them.

"You said you looked everywhere?"

"For days and weeks."

"You told me before that you tried to contact the father's family in England. I assume you got the police involved as well?"

"We informed the police, but they aren't much to speak

120   Patrick Tarr

of around here, especially with the war on. And yes, we wrote several letters to the Hawksbys—who were not close with the children's parents as I understand it, or at least not as close as Theresa was with her sister. They never replied. I assumed they'd died, or that they had their own problems and simply weren't interested."

"They claim not to have heard a word about the children since they left London. I can assure you, they're very interested in what has become of Frances and Michael."

"Where were they when the bombs were falling, then? Why send the children here?"

This wasn't Simon speaking, but Theresa. She stood at the door to the dining room, leaning on the frame. The sound of her voice startled Simon, but not me, because I'd seen her approach. Theresa gave her husband a hard look, then shifted her gaze to address me. There was a fierceness in her now, an edge that wasn't there when she'd first greeted me at my door.

"When Frances and Michael needed a new home, it was Simon and I who came forward to take them in. We've never had word from the Hawksbys. And if our letters to them didn't arrive, we likely have German U-boats to thank for that. Poor Frances and Michael lost their parents, and Simon and I lost our dear son Gerald before the war began . . . It seemed just right that my dear younger sister's children would come live with us, and make a new family out of those of us left. We were so pleased when those young ones arrived. Make no mistake, it broke our hearts when they ran away. Even though they were some trouble at times . . ."

Simon started to cry then, softly shaking his shoulders as he lowered his face into his hands. A low moan came out of him as he hunched over, shrinking into himself. His sorrow seemed to annoy Theresa. I saw her jaw clench as she looked away from him. Despite the revelation about their late son, the whole show struck me as false. Simon had even warned me in advance when we left the dining room that tears would be forthcoming.

"I'm sorry about your boy," I said. I looked from Theresa to Simon and back again. "How did he die?"

"He drowned."

"What a terrible thing."

"Yes." Theresa nodded, then balled up a fist and struck her chest. "Grief opens a door to the darkness, right in the very heart of you, that you can never close again."

I felt a little sorry for Theresa and Simon then, but I couldn't bring myself to trust them, or the stories they were telling me.

Theresa continued, as Simon wiped his tears. "We found him at Glass Bay, on the beach. He knew he wasn't supposed to go there alone. We'll never know why he disobeyed us."

"You said that you searched for Frances and Michael. You searched the water, I assume, and all over these woods?"

"As best we could. The wilds are vast, we're surrounded by Crown lands. We called and called until our voices were

122   Patrick Tarr

hoarse. The police looked around the area as well, brought their dogs out, put up some notices, but . . . I'm quite sure some misfortune befell them out there."

I wrote this down and thought of how I'd explain it all to my employer. I guessed he wouldn't like how it sounded. I didn't like it myself.

"I'm sure the Hawksbys will be upset by this news," I said. "A whole family gone. And these unfortunate children were sent away to be safe."

Simon pulled his hands away from his face then. He brought one of his fists down on the table. I didn't react, except to glance at an abandoned cup, which had shaken and spilled weak tea that leaked through the gaps in the slatted wood to drip onto the floor. There was sand on the floor in here too. Maybe all the resort's brooms had disappeared along with the children.

Staring at me now with naked hostility, Simon's nostrils flared as he breathed. Theresa remained in the doorway, still and impassive.

"Why do you suppose the children ran away?" I asked.

"They were homesick," Theresa said before Simon could speak. "Some nonsense about wanting to go back to London. I don't think poor Michael ever accepted that his parents were dead. We didn't take them seriously enough, I'm afraid. We truly didn't believe they'd go. But we treated them kindly. Very kindly, like they were our own. They were all I had left of my sister. The only blood family I had left. My own parents passed some time ago. But the children

THE GUEST CHILDREN

were so wilful and strange, we couldn't protect them from themselves."

"I'm sure it's difficult to talk about. I can take this back with me right away, but I doubt it's the last you'll hear of it. You mentioned something about a man with a boat?"

"Lazlo," Theresa said. "We pay him to bring us supplies over from his cabin on Lake Carver. It's not a motorboat, just a canoe. But he should be here tomorrow or the next day."

Simon curled his lip then, though I wasn't sure he knew he was doing it. "Unless you'd like to try the trail through the woods again, you'll have to spend the night with us. But we won't charge you for the room, seeing as you're not staying by choice."

"Well, thank you for your hospitality."

I rose to leave then. There were more questions to ask and more places to look, but I knew I'd get no further with these two today. But one thing did occur to me as I passed Theresa in the doorway to go back to my room and think it over.

"What about the others?"

"What others?" Theresa said. Her eyes widened as she said it, which struck me as odd considering what a harmless question it was.

"The other guests. Were any of them here when the children disappeared?"

"Oh, I see," she said. "I'm not sure I recall."

That seemed odd, but I let it go for the moment. "I

124   Patrick Tarr

understand the resort has closed. Do the guests still pay for their rooms?"

"They used to, but not anymore . . . They each have their roles pitching in around here. Cleaning, gathering firewood, and the like. We're in it together these days, I suppose you'd say."

"That's what these war years have been all about, haven't they? Doing one's part," Simon added.

"Such tragedy. So many lives lost, so many maimed and broken," Theresa said. Then she added, with a smile that pulled her features taut, "Thank goodness you seem to have come through it all right. Not a scratch on you, as far as I can see."

It was intended to get a rise out of me, so I didn't let it. "Like you said, we've all done our part in our own ways. I'm going to go tidy my things, and then I'll have a look around the grounds. If you don't mind."

Simon sat up straighter. "Why should we mind?"

"You're more than welcome," Theresa said. "In fact, you can invite the whole Hawksby family over to have a look for themselves whenever it suits them."

"Maybe I'll do just that."

"Don't wander too far," Simon said. "If you get lost again, I fear we won't find you. And do stay away from Glass Bay. Those old wooden stairs are rotted, and you're likely to break your neck getting down to the beach."

"That inlet with the small beach, you mean, with the

THE GUEST CHILDREN   125

playhouse? I've been there already," I said. "I came across it on my way here."

Theresa regarded me for an uncomfortably long moment, as Simon wiped his eyes on the sleeve of his shirt. "Did you," she said. "Then I suppose you're doubly fortunate we found you in one piece. Try not to waste that good luck. Stay close to the lodge."

I couldn't imagine what she meant by that. As I went out, Theresa moved to join Simon at the table. I heard their low whispers, but not what they were saying. When I glanced back, Theresa was bent over her husband, and they were both looking at me.

★ ★ ★

CHAPTER 19

It was a strange conversation, full of odd reactions and evasions. I ran through it again as I looked more closely at the photos on the lobby walls, taken at the resort when it was still open and flourishing. There were photographs from the 1920s and earlier, so I assumed Simon and Theresa must have taken the place over from previous owners. In all the photos, there was a sense of hope and joy in the guests' smiling faces. Maybe it was the war, or maybe it was something else, but I didn't think anyone had smiled like that in this place for a long time.

Beyond the lobby, opposite the dining area, there was a cramped billiards parlour next to the ballroom. Here, it smelled of mildew and old smoke. There were bruise-dark landscape paintings on the wall, which all looked to be the work of a single artist. The landscapes were of a piece with the terrain around the lodge, the same striated sheets of Canadian Shield rock and the towering trees of northern forests. Despite the natural beauty, something struck me as

THE GUEST CHILDREN

ghastly about the paintings. On a closer look, I realized it was just the yellowish tinge left behind by old cigars. It almost looked as if the canvases were sweating.

When I came back out of the billiards room, I peered around and saw that Simon and Theresa had left the screened porch. The reception area was empty. Quietly, I opened the door of the ballroom and walked across the swelled parquet floor to the other door I'd seen earlier.

The cloakroom was windowless and dark. There was a light switch on the wall, but I'd already worked out that the lodge hadn't had electricity in some time. Maybe they never had it at all but they'd put the wiring in anyway, hoping for a connection to civilization that never came. I could see two small suitcases at the back in the light coming from behind me. There was a sideboard on the opposite wall of the ballroom, and I went over to find a book of matches and a candle. I lit the candle and went in.

There were parallel hanging racks on each wall abutting shelves for luggage. A few old coats, likely belonging to current or former guests, drooped on hangers at the far end. There was water damage in the far corner, and one wall had a hole in the plaster like someone had put a fist through it. When I got to the suitcases, I held the candle out for a better look. The cases had numbered tags, just like the ones I'd seen with the children outside the train station.

The tags on the cases bore the names of Michael and Frances Hawksby.

128   Patrick Tarr

I opened Michael's first. There were some changes of clothing, a gas mask, a piece of what looked like shrapnel, some children's books—including *Five Children and It*, but not the same printing of the book I'd shared with my brother. There was a child's drawing of a stuffed bear with the name *Stanley* written under it. Inside a smaller kit bag, I found a toothbrush and paste, small nail scissors, a compass, and a pocketknife. I'd had doubts from the start about the story Theresa and Simon told me about the children running away, but now I knew it was a lie. A boy running into the wilderness in a strange place, however rushed or foolhardy his plan, would bring along his compass, and would never forget his pocketknife.

In Frances's suitcase, again there were clothes and some toiletries. She had a small mirror and an empty packet of boiled sweets hidden in a pencil case. There was also a little leather-bound journal, but the pages were all blank and I could tell some had been torn out. Tucked in the back were travel documents for the Hawksby children. There was a folding picture frame with photographs of a man and woman. I had to assume they were the parents.

These children did not run away.

When I closed the cases and stood up from my crouch, I bumped against a coat on the hanging rack. Somehow, all the coats had moved along the rail, from the far end to right behind me, while I searched the children's belongings. I had an unnerving sense they were crowding me,

THE GUEST CHILDREN 129

surrounding me, but I saw something then that distracted me before I gave it any real concern.

There was another hole in the wall, in the far corner near the door, right where the coats were hanging before they'd moved. The opening was small, maybe one foot square, at the base of the wall where it met the cloakroom floor. Taking the candle over to investigate, I crouched again and held the light to the darkness inside the cavity.

There was a little space in the wall there. Inside were a few sweets wrappers, some marbles, and some drawings tacked to the wall. A hiding spot, much like one we'd had in our room at the farm to keep things away from the prying eyes of Mrs. Sturgess. I took a closer look at the drawings. One was of trees, just hundreds and hundreds of stick trees with yellow-green tops all crowded up against each other. The other drawing was of a building, quite obviously Glass Point Lodge. They were just children's drawings, nothing special about either of them, until I pulled the lodge drawing off the wall and turned it over.

Michael and Frances Hawksby were here.

Not just that, there was some balled-up paper stuffed into the cavity. These pages were more than notes or drawings. There were several full pages covered in a child's attempt at tidy handwriting. As I started to read what was written on the crumpled paper, I heard footsteps somewhere nearby, so I decided to take the pages with me and get out of there.

Pushing the coats back down the rail to hide what I'd found, I blew out the candle and went to look around outside. I went out the rear lobby doors to a stone terrace, overgrown with weeds and lopsided with age. Outside, it was overcast, the sky a charcoal haze and a little mist on the water as the temperature shifted. There were a few tables and some lounge chairs under a pergola covered in some rampant climbing vine. The sun umbrellas were tattered, and one lay on its side tucked against the stone knee wall at the end of the terrace. Beyond the terrace was a garden. A stone path led down the slope of the garden towards the boathouse, a dock, and a small piece of pebbly beach.

I could see Julian on the dock. He flicked a fishing rod, casting a lure out into the still water with his one hand, then tucked the end of the rod into some sort of brace attached to his belt. The water here was the same near-black brown I'd seen over at Glass Bay. I got a chill thinking about the inexplicable way I'd found myself there the day before, the strange dream of Edward and the woman's pale face under the water.

I didn't want to be alone any longer, so I went down to join Julian on the dock, trying not to hurry though I desperately wanted to drive the memory of that woman's face from my mind. As I went, I looked over the drooping garden to distract myself. It must have been quite something once, while in spring bloom. But now, in late summer, it was wilted and going brown. There were a few benches

THE GUEST CHILDREN

131

around, and the beds were bordered with multicoloured stones. A thin stream ran down from the woods to the lake at the far edge of it.

When I got to the dock, Julian was casting again. He didn't look at me, but greeted me by name as I approached. He was focused on something—whether it was the fish or avoiding conversation with me, I couldn't be sure. I got my first full view of Blank Lake then, maybe a quarter mile across and a little under a mile long. There were no other signs of habitation, just a wall of trees and sloping stone right up to the water line.

"What do you catch here?" I asked.

"Pike, mostly. Good fish, but horribly bony. And we've got no good knives for filleting, although the ones we do have I try to keep sharp. One of the ways I do my part. Provisions have been scarce, so we eat the little fish too. I don't care for them myself."

"Have you been here long?"

Julian looked at me then, teasing his lure a little as he did. "I came up to Glass Point going on a year and a half ago. Used to holiday here with my late wife in the twenties. It was quite a place back then. Wasn't intending to stay when I returned, but I got stuck. There wasn't much to pull me back to where I'd come from."

Sitting down on the dock, I took off my shoes and socks, and put my sore feet in the cool water. I couldn't see an inch beyond them. Below me it could have been a foot deep or a hundred. I hoped that if I stayed there for a while,

132 Patrick Tarr

Julian would keep talking. I'd learned during my short time in the security job that people were more likely to tell you what you wanted to know if you didn't ask them about it directly, or if you didn't say anything at all.

Julian hummed. It was a gentle melody, and the tune was familiar to me, but I couldn't put my finger on it.

"What is that?"

"An old one, a very old one from the last war."

"Is that where you . . . ?"

"I lost my hand after my discharge, some years after the war. Crushed in an automobile accident. Sometimes I can find that a little funny. At least now that it's a long way behind me."

"You seem to get along all right."

"Do I?" Julian cast again and looked down at me sitting next to him. "You were smart not to enlist, you know. You would've died over there. I can tell that just by looking at you. Every new boy who came into the trenches, I could tell. I was never wrong."

I didn't know what to say in response to that, so we remained in silence for a while. There was a noticeable lack of birds about, and an oppressive hush over the landscape, until a single fish leapt far out on the lake.

When I'd waited long enough to change the subject, I asked, "Were the Hawksby children still living here when you arrived?"

"Oh no, they were long gone by then."

THE GUEST CHILDREN   133

I watched his float bob once, but nothing bit. He frowned, then teased the line before he continued.

"They ran away, as I'm sure you've heard. Probably died in those woods, much as it breaks my heart to say. I should think they're still out there. No marker, no proper burial. It's an awful shame, and that's all there is to say. It's easy to get lost here, as you saw for yourself."

"Did you not wonder why they'd ever do such a foolhardy thing? Weren't they warned about the dangers of those woods?"

Julian reeled his lure back in, pinched off the bait, and tossed it into the water. I watched the piece of earthworm floating on the surface, waiting for something to snatch it away.

"I don't wonder why people do things," he said. "You'll never make sense of it." He flashed a smile, with a few missing teeth. "It's pleasant to have a new face here."

We sat there for a while longer. When my sore feet felt better, I reached for my shoes and socks. "This boat, the one that brings supplies. It'll come tomorrow?"

"Tomorrow. The day after. I hope tomorrow. We're in need of many things."

I tied my shoes and stood up. From somewhere inside, I could hear someone playing a violin. It broke the pall of silence and carried over the water, bouncing back from the rock faces across the lake. Whoever was playing it was skilled, however mournful the music.

"Who's that playing?"

"Agatha. Quite good, isn't she? She can sing and dance as well. Used to be on the stage. She was here at the same time as the children, if I remember correctly. She's been here longer than any of us, apart from Simon and Theresa."

As he spoke, Julian pointed to an upstairs window. I hadn't looked back to the lodge itself yet. It was quite grand in its day, I imagined, with its grey stone and big timbers. The windows facing the water were all large, but mostly covered with closed curtains or ringed with climbing vines. The building had a sloped, shingled roof, mossy in places and peeling in others.

I couldn't tell if it was a casual thing Julian had told me about Agatha, or if he was purposefully directing me to someone who might be able to tell me more about the Hawksbys. I bade him goodbye and headed up to the lodge.

When I went back through the lobby, Theresa was behind the front desk counting candles from a cardboard box. I could have sworn I'd heard her speaking to someone just before I entered, but she was alone. She smiled quickly when I came in, as if the strange scene between the three of us in the screened porch had never happened.

"How do you like the lodge? We can't quite seem to keep up with the maintenance, but it's a beautiful setting, is it not?"

"I've never seen a spot quite like it."

"That's why it caught our eye. I'd always wanted to

THE GUEST CHILDREN

own an inn, and Simon was eager to leave his post in Ottawa. Terrible colleagues he had there. This was the fall of '35. We got the property for a song. It was a lumberman's summer residence before it became an inn after the First World War. We had guests who'd come up for long stays during the summer. Very well-to-do. But once the war began, they stopped coming. Bad timing for us."

I wasn't sure why Theresa was so forthcoming now after her thinly veiled hostility earlier, but she seemed determined to change the tune between us.

"I'm sure you'd like something to do while you're here," she said. "Simon and I play euchre with Julian and Agatha most afternoons. One of them would be more than happy to let you sit in—"

"That's fine, thanks. I'm just going to head upstairs to get some rest."

I could feel Theresa's eyes on me as I went up the curved stairs and back to my room. The violin had stopped by the time I reached the second floor. I was going to try to speak with Agatha, but before I got to her door, Helena emerged from her room at the far end of the hall. She beckoned to me, and I followed the carpet runner down to speak with her.

"Do you have a moment, Mr. Sturgess?"

"Of course."

I was surprised when Helena invited me into her room, even more so when she closed the door behind us. The room was a touch bigger than mine, but equally musty and in need of repairs. While mine looked out over the lake, hers looked out over the forest. She'd drawn some strange characters on the window glass with what looked like dark lipstick. Sensing my uncertainty, she took a small step backwards.

"I don't mean to be improper. I only wanted to speak in private."

"What can I do for you?"

Helena bit her lip then whispered, "You are planning to leave soon, yes?"

"As soon as I can."

"I would also like to leave here."

"You say that as if it's not possible."

Helena looked at me gravely, her skin pale in the light from the window. I saw raised red scratches on her arms, poking out from under the sleeves of her dress. Catching my look, she pulled the sleeves down further.

"It's nothing. The insects. One of the reasons I'd like to go."

"Will the boat not come tomorrow?" I asked.

"I can't say for certain."

Before I could ask her to explain, Helena looked to the window. Frowning, she went to close the curtains before she came back and clutched my arm. What light there was left gleamed in her wide eyes when she spoke.

"Those children . . . such tragedy. To lose so much, and brave so much, only to find themselves *here* . . ." She said the last word with derision, bordering on disgust.

The Guest Children

137

"If you dislike it so, why have you stayed?"

Helena smiled at me then, a sad smile she tried to disguise as a real one. "I haven't had anywhere better to go. And it is so beautiful around the lodge. But to confess the real reason, I must admit I've been hiding from the war. Now that it's over, it's time to stop hiding."

"Will you return to Austria?"

"To Europe, yes. As soon as I can. To Austria, I think no. I'd never feel safe again."

Helena looked out the window towards the forest. I wanted to ask what was written on the windowpanes but decided against it.

"I'd like to find out more about what happened to the children," I said. "Is it true that Agatha was here when they disappeared? Julian told me so."

"I couldn't say. We don't talk about that time."

"You don't talk about it at all?"

"Why would we? It's awful."

I looked to the door. "I think I'll go see her anyway. See what she remembers."

Helena motioned to the clock on her dresser, although I noticed it was stopped. "Go later. She'll be asleep now. Agatha drinks in the mornings and falls back to sleep until lunch." She offered a small shrug. "We all pass the time in our own ways."

"Well then, good to speak to you, Helena."

"To you as well."

Before I left the room, Helena cleared her throat. I

turned around and she had one hand up in the air. "May I suggest that you stay on the grounds? You should avoid going to the woods again. Especially to Glass Bay. It's just so easy to get lost."

"So I've been told."

"I know we must seem strange, all of us here."

"You've been on your own a long time, haven't you. I know what it's like to spend too long in the same company."

She smiled, a little too broadly. "I'm glad you understand."

"I'll see you at lunch?"

"We don't gather for lunch anymore. Theresa puts out some bread and preserves in the kitchen, and some tea."

"Well then, I'll see you at supper."

Before I left, I told her once again that I was sorry for the loss of her husband. She nodded, gripped my arm once more, and thanked me. I left her room then and went back down the hall to my own. It was midday, but as quiet as the middle of the night in the lodge. It felt as though people were hiding from me, even when I was speaking to them.

With Agatha sleeping it off for a while, I thought I should look at the pages I'd found in the cloakroom. It was time to see what Frances and Michael Hawksby had to say for themselves.

★　★　★

CHAPTER 20

Although I'd found the empty journal in Frances's suitcase, the torn-out pages seemed to bear Michael's handwriting. In the first entries, he wrote only of the trials of their journey away from home, and of missing his lost parents. The boy seemed to hold a belief that, some way or another, he'd see them again. I read all about their Atlantic crossing from Liverpool, the U-boat attack on their convoy, and the various temperaments of the other children on board.

Michael reported that he was seasick for much of the journey. After meals, he'd lean over the rail and throw up until there was nothing left. It upset him because the meals were good, and it wasn't fair to lose them. He missed Stanley, who I assumed was the stuffed bear by the same name I'd seen in his drawing downstairs. Michael worried for his bear, adrift in the ocean with bodies, oil spills, and people's sick. Losing Stanley made him as sad as losing his parents.

Frances wasn't seasick like her brother, and Michael thought she looked cross with him for having such a hard time, which he also felt wasn't fair. He had no more control over his tummy than he did over the war, after all. He reported that most of the other children on board the ship were girls, and nasty girls at that. They teased him for crying about his lost bear, but they stopped when Frances told them about their mum and dad.

When Michael wasn't throwing up, he liked to watch the Dutch sailors on board, who in their spare time would make clogs out of hunks of wood. They sold some to the passengers and gave a few pairs away. Michael wanted a pair for himself, but he was too shy to ask the tall, blond, suntanned men to make him some.

There were meals, and drills, and meals, and drills. From time to time they sang more songs or were read stories. They were reminded daily that they were English Guest Children, and therefore ambassadors of their nation. One chaperone told them that if they behaved well during their stay overseas, perhaps more Canadian men would volunteer to help win the war so they could return to their homes and their parents. Michael raised his hand when the chaperone said that. He was disappointed that he was never called upon to speak.

I read on, skimming over their arrival in Newfoundland, where they saw First World War–era American destroyers in the St. John's harbour. The warships had four funnels and looked quite old and bulky. Michael worried for them, because he didn't think they'd stand a chance if they went up against the U-boats in the vast Atlantic depths.

THE GUEST CHILDREN 141

In St. John's, they stayed up late to look at the lights. They'd not seen street lights in over a year. Michael thought they looked magical, and he was irritated that Frances didn't feel the same way. After she went to sleep, Michael stared up at the ceiling and tried to pretend it was the ceiling in their old bedroom, in their old house, and that everything was back to how it should be.

From St. John's they went on to Halifax, where they saw Canadian soldiers boarding a ship, preparing for a voyage of their own. They met new chaperones, and the children they'd travelled with all went in different directions. They got their physicals and vaccinations from a doctor with salt-and-pepper hair. Michael reported that the man smelled of peppermint and liniment. The doctor's hands shook with the stethoscope as he listened to Michael's racing heart.

For Michael, the worst part of it was all the questions. So many questions, and Michael had to keep telling people over and over that his mum and dad were dead by German bombs. Sometimes he told them about losing Stanley to the U-boats too, mostly because he just didn't want to talk about Mum and Dad anymore.

When they got on the train in the city of Halifax, Michael leapt under a seat when the whistle sounded, thinking it was an air-raid siren. A thin, red-faced man in a threadbare suit laughed aloud when Michael did that, but he stopped when he saw the sharp looks from other passengers. Michael wrote that he wished for a bomb to fall on that man's house, but he prayed for forgiveness that night and hoped it wouldn't come to pass. After they switched trains in Toronto to travel north towards the lodge, Michael described the landscape looming on either side of the train, so vast and so wild, like nothing he'd ever seen.

It was interesting to read the first impressions of a boy who'd never left London before this journey. He was older than Edward and me when we'd come over by a few years. I didn't remember anything about our life over there. I had no memories of the voyage, or even of our arrival at the Sturgess farm. The oldest memory I had was of hearing my brother getting the belt from Mr. Sturgess in the next room, while I waited in terror for my turn.

It was hard not to sympathize with Michael, who had to face so much so young, and was not built to handle such hardships. In his writings, he struck me as more than a little like my brother in his quiet strangeness, but without Edward's chaotic nature, or the toughness he'd had as a boy. Maybe he was what Edward might have been, had he not taken so many blows in life.

As I read on, Michael wrote that he hoped they'd see grizzly bears and wolves, or at least sled dogs like he'd read about in *The Call of the Wild* and other adventure stories. But he didn't see anything from the train, apart from some circling birds too high to make out.

After it turned dark, Michael made a wish upon the moon and on each new star he saw in this vast new sky. He wished to see his parents again, no matter what he had to give up to do it. Michael knew his wish could never come true, but as

THE GUEST CHILDREN   143

he travelled ever northward in that untamed place, he dearly wanted to believe that anything was possible.

The next entry after this was several days later. By that point, the children had arrived at Glass Point Lodge and met their aunt and uncle there. The man piloting the boat sounded just like Mr. Schust, and I wondered why the old man would have lied to me about meeting them. Michael's first impressions of the resort were tinged with disappointment that there were no other children about. There were all the rules as well. Rules about being quiet. Rules about mealtimes, study times, and sleep time. Rules about where they could and couldn't go.

At first, they were forbidden from exploring the forest and shoreline. Michael resented this, although he wrote more than once about a frightful feeling that sometimes came over him looking out the lodge windows at the wilds. He didn't like how much Theresa looked like his mother, and he was plainly frightened by his uncle Simon's mood swings.

The entry from their third day at Glass Point Lodge was where things started to get strange. As I read on, my grip tightened on the paper.

I woke up again. There was sand in my bed, even more than before, and I heard someone calling to me. It wasn't the high-sounding voice from before, not the Wet Boy who stood at the edge of the woods waving at me last night. I want to go play with him, but not in the dark. I've seen things in the forest, even in the day-time. Sometimes they are such dreadful things. But I know the trick to them. Close my eyes and look away. Then when I open, they're gone. The Wet Boy doesn't scare me, but I wonder why he won't say hello to me during the day, even though I see him sometimes watching me from the trees or from under the water.

The voice tonight didn't sound real like the Wet Boy's, and it was more like I heard it in my head than in my ears. I went downstairs and out the back door so I could see who it was, but didn't go any closer to the forest. Again I saw someone wave to me from the tree line. This time it didn't look like a person at all, he was too big and had a funny shape. I heard the voice again, a deep friendly voice, asking me to come out and play.

Whoever it was, he made another wave for me to follow him into the trees. I think he wanted me to go to Glass Bay, but I didn't want to, not with a stranger. It's not that I was frightened. It's just that all the things that make me want to close my eyes are there. I'm not a brave boy, as Frances has told me, but I am not a coward either.

When I went back to our room, I tried to wake Frances, but she didn't stir. I looked out the window again, but the strange figure was gone. I started thinking about Mum and Dad and how they hadn't found us yet. Then I started to cry. I didn't want to, but I'm a crybaby too, on top of not being brave. I knew that if Frances woke up, she'd be cross with me, or that if Simon heard me, he'd shout at me the way I hear him shouting downstairs at night sometimes. I know I shouldn't talk about the things I've seen. They'll only think I'm pretending. It's lonely here, worse than school or being at sea. I think being lonely is the worst thing, even worse than what's outside.

THE GUEST CHILDREN   145

There were no more written pages after that, just a few scribbled drawings of trees and distant figures. The boy had some bad dreams in his first days at the resort, that much was clear. It was yet another thing we had in common. But with the mention of such strange visions—a wet boy and a strange, waving figure in the forest—it was hard to tell if Michael was suffering delusions as a result of his grief and isolation, or just making up stories to entertain himself.

It did seem that it wasn't just me who sensed there was something wrong with this place, something unnerving about the woods around us, and some kind of darkness in Simon.

In his final entry, he'd written about Glass Bay. I'd been warned more than once not to go there, but there was no question in my mind now that I had to go back to that beach. I'd found the first of Michael's notes on the stairs there, after all. Maybe I'd missed something.

Rising from the bed, I looked out my window and saw Julian still in his spot on the dock. I thought I saw someone swimming in the opaque water, but it must have been a trick of the light, because no one ever surfaced. Standing there, I decided it was time to go back along the trail to Glass Bay. It was early enough in the day yet, and I still needed answers to bring back with me. It couldn't be too far. I figured if I stayed close to the shoreline, I'd be able to find it again without too much trouble.

If they hadn't all told me not to go there, maybe I would have left it alone.

CHAPTER 21

I walked out the back of the building and headed for the tree line. Off by the boathouse, Simon was chopping wood. He was unsteady on his feet as he swung, swaying when the axe arced high. I thought him far more likely to return to the lodge missing half a foot than he was to produce a bundle of kindling. He took a long time between swings, and I could see him panting.

I'd only been watching a moment when he jerked his head back to look at me. I waited to see if he'd wave. He only stood there looking at me and breathing hard, so I kept walking. He swung the axe again, and I heard him curse about something in a hiss of breath.

Nearby, there was a gravel path I started to follow, weedy and weather-damaged, unmaintained for some time. When I got to the edge of the forest, a faded sign pointed to Glass Bay. I spotted the trailhead, but stood rooted in the daylight at the gateway to the wilderness, thinking about my trip through those same woods the day before. I

The Guest Children 147

questioned my resolve to retrace steps I couldn't remember taking in the first place.

Before long, I managed to force myself into motion, thinking of the children—and of Edward, still alone and liable to become trouble for me before long. I started along the trail, walking over black, muddy ground, already feeling the pain in my blistered feet.

It was still overcast, and there was mist in the air as I walked along the trail. It was dank in this part of the forest, despite the supposed recent lack of rain—a hushed place of moss and toadstools, and felled trees in rot. There was deadfall all around, choked in climbing vines.

The path went over and around ridges of exposed rock, and there were more of those cracks and crevasses waiting to break an ankle or swallow me whole. Swarms of mosquitoes buzzed around my face. I swatted them away for a while, thinking of the scratches on Helena's arms, but after a time I gave up and let them have at me. Before long, I noticed the woods didn't seem as threatening as they had on my first hike in from the road, although there was still an unpleasant character to the place. I felt foolish for my panic and the bewildering fugue of the day before. A lack of food and water was the most likely cause for those unsettling visions.

Lost and alone, old bad memories returned in a landscape that reminded me of my childhood, that was all it was. But as I continued along the trail, more whispers of the previous day came back to me. The way that shack quivered when I approached. Young Edward running past me in the woods. The woman gazing up at me from under the water. The deeper I trudged into the forest, the more these memories swam back, and the less sure I was about the journey.

As I thought about turning around, I heard and felt what sounded like a heavy tree falling somewhere close by—first the surprised protest of cracking branches, and then a powerful, thundering crash that reverberated through the sheet of solid rock under my feet. I felt it in my bones. It was such an overwhelming sound that I needed to see the aftermath for myself.

Where the trail curved inland from the raised and rocky shoreline of the bay to my right, I came to a hollow in the landscape. The tree lay directly across my path, its massive trunk broken into sodden, moss-covered pieces. The soil on either side of the path was waterlogged. The stream that fed into the lake must have gathered some of the runoff from here.

Instead of treading through the muck, I tried climbing over the trunk, some three feet around. But as I stepped atop it, the decomposing log gave out under my weight, breaking apart beneath me in a tumult of soft, damp rot, of squirming and scuttling things. I fell headlong onto the path on the other side, my face impacting the damp soil before my arms could break the fall.

When I raised my head from the ground, I was somewhere else again.

THE GUEST CHILDREN

149

I was back on the Sturgess farm, lying on a frigid patch of rock, snow-laden spruce boughs just over my head. I was freezing, shivering hard, but for some reason I wasn't moving to keep warm. I could feel the cold burning into my fingertips where they touched the stone. About to climb to my feet, I heard people close by. When I saw who it was, I stayed still.

Mr. Sturgess stood over my brother, his black leather belt flashing against the snow-covered yard out back of the farmhouse. Edward, his bare torso red from the cold and redder still in long welts across his back from the belt, was silent. Mr. Sturgess spooled his belt around his fist and leaned down to say something to Edward. In response, my brother threw up in the snow.

I remembered why this was happening. I remembered the day Mrs. Sturgess found the neighbour's stolen liquor in Edward's hidey-hole. When she showed it to Mr. Sturgess, he went quiet. Edward gave me a dark smile, but he couldn't hold on to it against the fear. Before the punishment came, Edward told me not to take any of the blame, that it was his doing and he'd pay for it himself. I didn't tell him that I'd never even considered the thought.

After Mr. Sturgess went back to the house, leaving Edward there in the cold, I went to help him. I draped his coat over him, eased him back to the house, and half carried him up to our room. He wasn't crying any longer, didn't make a sound as I put him into his bed. At one point, on the stairs, I looked back and saw Mrs. Sturgess at the bottom.

She didn't speak, and she didn't help. She just watched us for a moment, blankly, and then moved on.

I went back down with an old shirt and filled it with snow. Wrapping it up tight, I went back up and pressed the shirt against Edward's welts until he told me to leave it alone. There was another jar of the stolen liquor Mrs. Sturgess hadn't found, and he asked me to give him some. Watching the door and listening for footsteps in the hall, I did.

After he had some, Edward seemed a little better. The fear went away. That usual cunning sheen came back into his eyes. I told him to take it easy for a while, to keep his head down and stay out of the way, but he wasn't having it.

"I think I could kill him," he said after a while. "I know I could."

"No, you couldn't. You saw what he did."

"We'd have to be clever."

"I don't want to."

"Yes, you do. You want it even more than me."

Edward was right. I dreamed of the death of Mr. Sturgess at night, and through most of my days too. My brother took the worst from him, but I got it as well, and usually when I'd done less to deserve it. I knew how strong the man was, and how vicious. I tensed up just at the sight of his shadow crossing our doorway.

"I hate him too."

I hadn't heard the door creak when I said it, but I saw Edward's eyes flit to the space behind my back. There were

THE GUEST CHILDREN   151

two heavy footfalls on the plank floor, and then I was rising so fast, a strong hand clenched around my neck. Flung into the corner, I didn't have time to put my hands out, and my face struck the wall so hard I felt my nose break.

I came back to my senses coughing up water.

Soaked through, my hands were clutching sand. I could feel the raw grit of it in my mouth as I raised myself up from the shallows. I wasn't in the Sturgess house anymore. I wasn't even in the forest anymore.

Once more, I was on the beach at Glass Bay.

Those rickety wooden stairs led up the rock face in front of me. The raised playhouse at the end of the beach stood there watching, strips of burlap in the windows not moving at all despite the breeze on my wet skin. I realized now that the playhouse was in fact Glass Point Lodge poorly built in miniature. As I regarded it, I saw movement behind the burlap.

"Is someone there?"

Wading towards the shore, not ready to confront the fact that once again I'd come to this beach without meaning to, without even remembering the journey, I kept my eyes on the playhouse. There was no answer, and I saw no further movement as I drew close. Dripping lake water onto the sand, I kicked off my shoes and approached the back side of the structure.

There was a three-rung ladder to get to the platform, and the engraved lettering I'd seen only from a distance before, which read *THE SAND PALACE*.

It was dim inside the structure as I climbed up and onto the platform. A strange choice to blot out daylight in a children's playhouse. I pushed the burlap curtains aside, wrapping them around the window frames to let the light in. There wasn't much to see. The structure was rough and thrown-together on the inside. There were jagged cuts in the wood and the plank floor was uneven. Some of it was due to decay, but even the rapid construction of the temporary wartime houses looked like fine work compared with this. There were notches carved into the walls and floor with a knife, alongside some strange-looking figures and faces. There was also the damp outline of a human form, which could only be my own. It was not my first time inside this place.

I didn't like that feeling. Claustrophobia surged up in me, and I went to the window for air. From inside the small rendering of the lodge, I looked out at the water, then up the steep rock face to the tree line above me.

There were two children standing up there.

Not small children. Thirteen or fourteen at least, a boy and a girl. They were dirty, in threadbare and ill-fitting clothes, with stringy hair. They stood too near to the cliff edge, seemingly unfazed by the long drop to the rocks and water below. It could only be Frances and Michael Hawksby, and they were looking right at me.

"Hello!" I called out to them.

They didn't respond or move. I couldn't even be sure they were real.

THE GUEST CHILDREN

153

"Please stay where you are!"

Again, they didn't answer. Then the boy looked over his shoulder and nudged his sister. She too looked back, and then they both turned and vanished into the trees. I called out to them to stay, but they didn't. My surprised voice bounced back at me from the rocks.

The children couldn't just reappear after spending years missing in the forest, with no help, no communication with anyone until now. Surely, if they'd been around all this time, Simon and Theresa or the others would have seen them. Unless, of course, they were lying about the whole thing. It was the only thing I was certain about, that those two were lying.

Standing in the playhouse, I thought about racing up the wooden staircase to go after Michael and Frances, but I didn't want to rush on the rickety thing. Not to mention, the children would know the woods better than me, and they wouldn't be found unless they wanted to be. I could go out in search of them soon, but now was not the time.

My clothes were still damp as I went down the short ladder to the sand and crouched down. Beneath the structure was a mess of intercrossed spiderwebs, several of their makers perched there, fat and patient, as they waited for something to fly underneath the playhouse. I didn't like the look of them and quickly moved away.

A long and careful climb later, I was back up at the top of the bay and standing in the same spot where I'd seen the children. There was no sign of them now. No tracks in the ground. No vegetation disturbed. No more little notes left behind. Standing up there, I could see my own footprints along the beach and leading to and from the Sand Palace.

But there was something else I hadn't noticed when I was on the beach—more footprints, all around mine, in all kinds of lines and spirals. The footprints were most concentrated around the Sand Palace, which I could see from here was crooked and leaning a little to the right. It appeared the children had been down there too, watching me. The last thing I remembered, I'd been at the tree trunk, where I'd slipped into the clutches of bad memories. The children couldn't have carried me, so they must have followed me there, lost as I was in whatever trance state had urged me on. It was an awful feeling, thinking about being so helpless as that.

When I heard my name called out, my jump nearly sent me reeling over the edge. I stepped well back, breathless, and searched the woods behind me for the source of the voice. I saw Agatha standing on the trail some distance away, watching me with a drink in her hand.

"You've been gone a long time, they asked me to look for you."

I didn't think I'd been gone for long at all. My balance was shaky, my legs quivering with the chill from my damp clothes. Although I was now a good distance from the long drop to the rocks below, I still didn't feel safe. Agatha had stepped off the trail and approached me. Her arms were

THE GUEST CHILDREN   155

bony, but the hand that gripped my wrist to pull me back towards the trail was strong.

"You shouldn't stand near there, you could take a tumble," she said.

"I saw the children. They were right here."

Agatha looked at me and blinked. "Did you," she said.

"That's all you have to say?"

"They were right here, you say? The Hawksby children?"

"Yes."

"And where were you?"

"Down there. In the playhouse. Look, you can see their footprints."

Agatha peered over the edge of the cliff. "I can see footprints. Don't know whose. They could all be yours, no? You shouldn't be going down there."

"Did you hear what I said?"

"I heard you. You said you saw Michael and Frances. But tell me this—do you remember how you got down there? Or how you got through the forest yesterday?"

"No. I don't."

"Well then, how can you trust what you saw?"

"How could you know that I don't remember . . ."

"Apart from the children, have you been seeing other things, hearing other things?" Agatha made a fluttering gesture next to her own head as she said that. I couldn't tell if she was swatting at a bug or making a comment about my sanity.

"Why don't you tell me what's going on here, Agatha."

"Oh dear, nothing's *going on*. It's a place where you just . . . you can't trust your eyes and ears. Things get strange when you come out here. But please know this, it is all in your head."

"You're saying you've seen things too."

The ice cubes rattled in her glass. She rattled them further to make a point. "Less and less all the time. You could have died out here, Mr. Sturgess. Please understand that. Don't come out here alone again. You were warned for a reason."

"Have you ever seen Michael and Frances?"

"They're dead. As I'm sure you've already heard. It's not a nice thing to hear, but it must be true, and there's nothing we can do about it now. Millions dead from all that nonsense, we just have to add them to the list. Let's head back now. This isn't a good place for you."

"What does that mean?"

Agatha reached out for my face, wiping my nose with a handkerchief from my pocket that she handed to me when she was finished. I looked at the spot of red on the creamcoloured fabric and thought of the black marks I'd seen on the trees. I didn't even know my nose was bleeding, and I thought again of the night Mr. Sturgess threw me into the wall at the farm.

"Do you remember that happening to your nose?"

"No."

"Come on now, back to the lodge."

THE GUEST CHILDREN   157

Right then, more than anything, I wanted to be home. I longed for my hovel with Edward. At least, when I had nightmares there, I could be sure of where I'd wake up.

Agatha tugged on my sleeve and peered into my eyes. "Come on, I'll make us a drink in my room. I heard you have some questions for me."

She started walking without waiting for my reply. Before I followed her, I noticed movement just off the trail, and was transfixed at what I saw. Pale, fish-belly fingers scrambled up over the lips of a fissure in the stone. I tried to get a better look, but when I got closer, the fingers slid away. When I looked down into the deep slit of rock, I saw what looked like two pennies flashing sunlight at the bottom. The light from them went dark and then flashed again, something like the slow blink of a pair of eyes.

I'd seen enough now. I hurried to catch up to her.

★ ★ ★

CHAPTER 22

As we walked back along the Glass Bay trail, we were silent. Agatha kept stealing glances at me. She wore the kind of wide-legged trousers that had become popular since the war started, a white cotton blouse, and a rust-coloured cardigan. Her white hair was ornately braided down her back. I wondered who did that for her. As she moved along the trail with a grace that my clumsy steps couldn't match, her eyeglasses bounced on a chain around her neck. I felt Glass Bay behind me like cold breath on my neck, and wanted to shake off the memory of it.

"Julian told me you were an actress," I said.

"Actress, singer . . . dancer when I had to be."

"Do you miss it?"

"Parts of it, yes. Most of it, no."

We walked on for a while longer. As we went, I searched the landscape for the fallen tree I'd found right before everything went strange. I didn't see it. It seemed we were

The Guest Children

going back a different way from the way I'd come. Overgrown ghosts of trails led off in every direction. From one moment to the next, I couldn't have said which one would take us back to the lodge.

"Did you hear something before?" I asked. "A tree falling?"

"No."

"I find that hard to believe. The sound it made, I'd have thought they'd hear it all the way over at the marina."

She shrugged. "Sound travels funny in the woods."

Agatha watched her own feet navigating the crevassed rock and tree roots as she spoke. She seemed to know the trails remarkably well, considering all the warnings I'd had to stay close to the lodge. We went on in silence for a while. As we rounded a bend, she stopped and looked up into the trees for a moment before she got moving again. I tried to follow her gaze, but I saw nothing there.

"Tell me something," she said. "The children . . . When you thought you saw them just now, what did they look like?"

"They were dirty, unkempt. Something strange about them. They didn't respond when I called out. They just went back into the trees."

"I see. And how old did you say?"

"I don't know for sure. They were far away."

"It can't have been them."

"So you said."

"But do you believe me?"

I didn't see the point of lying about it. "I don't know who to believe."

Agatha nodded and leaned closer to me as we walked, too close. She whispered, "While you were out here, did you also see a woman . . . a pale woman with red hair?"

That caught me off guard. I wasn't sure whether I should tell her the truth about the woman I'd seen in the lake the day before, or about the mention of the Red Lady I'd seen in the pages of Michael's journal. But she had brought it up, not me.

"Not today. Yesterday, maybe . . ."

"Tell me where."

"In the water. Down at Glass Bay. Did I imagine that too?"

Agatha slowed her pace and looked at me. Her thin throat constricted as she swallowed, then she scanned our surroundings before she whispered, "Did she speak to you?"

"No."

"What was she doing?"

"Watching me? I don't know."

"I see."

"Do you know who she is?"

"Never mind."

Agatha was tall, nearly my height, and our faces were close together in the dim light of the forest. I wasn't sure how old she was, somewhere in her early sixties, I guessed, but her eyes were bright and sharp, and I could see the magnetism that must have drawn people to watch her perform—a faint but warm glow from somewhere deep inside her. I could also tell, because I knew what to look for in the way her eyes shifted and the way she carried herself, that she was lying to me.

"You must stay away from that beach. Just go back to the city, tell everyone who needs to know it that those poor children were lost. Let them mourn. There's nothing else for you here, nothing you want to find."

"More people will come here. You must know that. The truth will come out."

Agatha let out a short, brittle laugh. "That's not going to happen."

"What does that mean?"

Her face took on a new expression. I couldn't quite describe it, except that it felt like the first time she wasn't putting on some kind of performance for my benefit.

"Randall, do you believe in ghosts?"

"No. I don't think I do."

"Good. Then you'll find no ghosts here."

I didn't know how to take that, given that she'd been implying the opposite ever since she found me. "So, who is that woman to you?"

Agatha stopped in the forest so quickly I nearly ran into her. She turned slowly, her eyes scanning the woods.

"Don't talk about her."

"Why?"

Agatha shook her head. I noticed that there were no bird calls anymore. There were no squirrels or chipmunks about. Even the mosquitoes were gone. I was sure the silence was new, that just moments before there'd been the usual murmuring chaos of wood song.

Breathing in the damp air, I felt a droplet of water fall on the back of my neck. I almost shouted when it hit me. Agatha saw me flinch, and she smiled. It wasn't a kind smile.

"Are you afraid?"

"Should I be?"

"It doesn't make any difference one way or another."

"Why do you stay here?"

"That is a complicated question."

"No, it isn't."

"The reasons I have to stay are the same reasons you should go."

She started walking again, quickly, and I followed as best I could without tripping. "I don't understand."

"There's something I see in you, Randall. I don't know what it is, but things will be bad for you if you stay, and make no mistake."

I was growing tired of these people trying to intimidate me with vague pronouncements of doom. It was a diversion tactic, nothing more, as if I was getting closer to a truth they all wanted to hide from me.

"You were here when the children went missing. Is it

THE GUEST CHILDREN   163

true the police were brought in to look? Was the area searched like they told me?"

"There were police, yes, and some men with dogs. But the area is so vast, so wild . . . there was never any real hope of finding them."

"You met Frances and Michael. Did they have any reason to run away? Did their aunt and uncle mistreat them?"

"Well, no . . ."

"But?"

"They might have been better prepared for the dangers they would face. They didn't know that they weren't safe. They should have been told. That's the thing I can't condone."

Agatha stopped again on the trail. She was staring into the dense forest again as if she'd seen something, or someone. She shook her head then, as if communicating to whoever was out there. I shifted, trying to follow her line of sight. I saw what I thought was a flash of red, but then nothing else. The woods were still unnaturally quiet.

"Is there someone there now?"

Giving me a half smile, Agatha shook her head and started along the path back to the resort. I kept looking behind us, but I saw no one. Agatha stepped up her pace, speaking without looking back at me.

"Almost home now. Should be suppertime soon."

"Already?"

"We eat early and retire early. Without electricity,

there's not a lot to occupy ourselves with in the hours after dark. Tell me, do you have family?"

"I have a younger brother, he's my only blood."

"And where is he now?"

"In the city. I need to finish here and get back to him. He's unwell." I wasn't sure why I'd shared that, but it seemed to soften her towards me.

"I'm sorry to hear it. If I may, what is his affliction?"

"It's a complicated thing . . . But at the root of it all, I think, is an injury or an illness of the mind. There's nothing that can be done about it. He just needs taking care of, and that's fallen to me for most of my life."

I didn't know what Edward's condition was called, or even if he truly suffered from one, but it was easiest to describe it as such because most often it ended the conversation.

Agatha nodded. "I know how that goes. I loved someone who suffered from something like that. What the French called madness in two forms."

"What happened?"

"It's not a story for now."

As the trailhead came into view, with the tree-ringed lodge and Blank Lake beyond it, Agatha said, "When you have someone like that close to you, you have to accept that it is a struggle you may never win, but it is worth struggling all the same."

She walked ahead of me then, and I thought of Edward alone and restless in our room. I wondered what he was doing, right at that moment. Every possibility that came to mind filled me with unease.

Moving along the trail, we skirted the shoreline. The sun peeked through the clouds and beams of its light shone down on the waters of Blank Lake. Something jumped in the water, and I saw some bird of prey circling the trees on the far side of the lake.

It was a wild place, with a kind of unsettling beauty in its wildness, but there was that sour, mouldering smell underlying it all. An unpleasant scent of rot that reminded me of city slaughterhouses in the summer heat.

When we passed the boathouse, I peered inside. As I did, I thought I saw a figure shift in the shadows. I assumed it must be one of the others, but when I stopped and moved for a closer look, the figure retreated further into the dark, away from my sight.

As I went to step into the boathouse for a closer look, Agatha whistled for my attention. "Let's go indoors. You were out there a long time. And I promised you a drink."

"There's someone in the boathouse."

"What makes you think that?"

"I saw them."

"You saw shadows. No one goes in there anymore. We have no working boats. Come on now, it's better inside."

Agatha walked into the lodge before I could ask what she meant by that, but I wasn't swayed by her attempt to pull me away.

When I stepped into the boathouse, there seemed to be no one there. I smelled something, though. A human scent, unwashed and pungent, on top of the usual boathouse smells of oil, old rope, and damp lumber. I didn't like being alone in the hulking dark of the place and found I didn't have the nerve to speak out loud to confirm that I was alone.

Anyway, it was just a shadow, like Agatha said. Once my eyes had adjusted, I could see well enough to be sure I was alone. I turned back and followed Agatha into the lodge.

★　★　★

CHAPTER 23

I took Agatha up on the drink, which was some godawful kind of moonshine cut with water, along with a home-made herbal tonic she told me she made herself out of roots and plants from the garden. There was no ice at Glass Point, except in winter, so nothing to cut the taste, but the drink did loosen the knot I'd had cinched tight in my gut since the moment I got out of Schust's truck and started my walk through the woods.

Agatha was charming, and a good storyteller, but she only partly warmed my mistrust as she told me of her experiences in city playhouses and with touring companies in the old days. She spoke of another actress, one she deeply admired, who worked with her for a number of years. I noticed that her mood darkened at the end. She looked out her window towards the woods and drained her glass in one go.

Her room was brighter than mine, although she'd hung colourful translucent scarves from the ceiling that filtered

168   Patrick Tarr

and tinted the light. There were books scattered on the floor, and clothes draped on all the furniture. On a high shelf, she had three wooden heads displaying her best wigs.

Whenever I tried to turn the conversation back to the children or tried to learn more about the lodge and its inhabitants, she'd find a way to change the subject. She did it gracefully each time, but not so gracefully that I didn't notice it happening. She wanted to talk about the distant past only, it seemed. And so she did, always about her life before the lodge, before the war, before some other pivotal event in her life that she alluded to but never quite defined. However evasive, she appeared to be glad for my company—a new audience for her stories.

Once I realized I'd get no more out of her, I looked at the clock. Supper was soon, so I bade her farewell, and went back to my room to shave and change. The first thing I did when I got back was examine my suitcase. I could tell someone had gone through it because I'd put a little bit of paper next to the back hinge, and it had fallen out when they'd opened the case.

The pages from Michael's book were gone. So were the *Michael and Frances Hawksby were here* notes I'd found. It was Simon or Theresa—I was sure of that. They wanted something in the boy's writing to stay hidden from the family. I wondered what else they were hiding.

Taking my toiletry kit out, I fetched a bowl of water from a warm kettle in the empty kitchen. My face was still scratched up from my frantic afternoon in the woods the

THE GUEST CHILDREN 169

day before. Despite my usual tan from working outdoors, I looked sallow in the little mirror as I started to shave.

I thought again of Edward, who looked so much like me, though I'd been told more than once that he was just a little more handsome. He was always the one to catch a woman's eye first, only to lose it with his off-putting ways. I had to work harder than he did, but I'd had a few girlfriends before Mildred. Through them I learned it was better to keep my brother and my love life separate. He scared off three of them with fake stories about me before I got wise to what he was doing. Mildred wasn't going to meet Edward until later.

It was a later that never happened.

Worrying over him, I wished there was a telephone so I could call the apartment's shared line and pass on a message through Sybil or one of the other tenants. There was no way anyone could reach me at the lodge if anything went wrong. I doubted that our neighbours would even go to the trouble of trying to track me down. For all that I'd told myself I was doing this for the both of us, and for these children whose story was so like our own, I still couldn't deny that I'd done it, at least in part, to get away from him and from that room. I knew Edward would be overwrought by now, watching the peepholes for intruders and jittering with paranoia.

Sometimes, I wondered if my brother's vigilance wouldn't have served him well in the war. A sentry, a sniper, a scout—his watchful caution might have made him a useful soldier. But his fearfulness would have been crippling. That had started more recently—only after the war began—and was so out of character with the Edward I'd always known.

That fearless boy I remembered was the one watching Mr. Sturgess through the farmhouse curtains on the day he told me what he planned to do to set us free from the farm. Ever since our encounter with the man in the woods, and what Mr. Sturgess had done to him, Edward's thinking had shifted. He had this new idea that killing was easy, and that it was the answer to our problems.

I didn't want anything to do with his plans. I still feared Mr. Sturgess, just as we always had until that point. We weren't strong enough to take him on, and that was that.

"We can poison him. He'll die before he knows what hit him."

"What about *her*?"

Edward shrugged. It was clear enough to me what the shrug meant. He wanted Mrs. Sturgess gone too.

"No," I said.

"Has she ever protected us from him?"

"We don't know, do we."

"We don't know, because she hasn't."

I hoped he was going to forget about it, but he didn't. He kept whispering to me in the night, after the lights were out. He spooled out plans for Mr. Sturgess, moving from poison to fire to drowning, usually landing on bludgeoning him in the bed where he slept just down the hall. I asked him to stop sometimes, begged him sometimes too. Usually, by the time I fell asleep, Edward was still killing Sturgess, still whispering, and those whispers followed me down.

When I looked away from the wall mirror, I noticed there was sand in the basin I'd used for shaving. I ran a hand through my hair and more fell into the water. I remembered Michael writing about the sand in his bed, and I noticed something then that I hadn't seen when I'd first returned to the room. There was sand on the windowsill too, a thin and perfect layer of it. I ran a finger across it and looked closer. It was fine and dark, like the sand on the beach at Glass Bay. I'd never seen any quite so dark in colour.

When I brushed it away, it fell to the floor with the same eerily musical sound I'd heard before. Trying the window, I found it locked and shut tight, so it was unlikely the sand had blown through the crack. But it had to have come from somewhere.

As I looked up to the ceiling for the source, the ringing of a high bell downstairs startled me. Time for supper, which I imagined would involve more suspicious behaviour from my hosts. Exiting my room, I nearly bumped into Helena, coming down the hall from her own. Her dress was wrinkled now and her eyes were red. She looked tired.

"Are you all right?"

"Yes, fine. Just feeling a bit blue."

"Sorry to hear that."

"It's just what we talked about before. After all this time, it's hard to think of leaving."

"I understand."

I didn't, though. I couldn't comprehend how anyone would miss Glass Point Lodge, but I wasn't there to understand such things. If there was a way to find out more about the children over dinner, I would. But by that point, any further answers I'd get didn't seem as important as they had earlier. I already had more than enough to take back with me to the family's lawyer.

Michael and Frances were missing and had been presumed dead for a long time. Returning to the city with that information represented the extent of the job I'd been hired to do. After the events of that afternoon, all I wanted was for that boat to arrive and take me back to civilization, where I could share this highly suspect situation with the man who hired me, then get paid and go home flush enough to keep a roof over our heads for a while.

The Hawksby family could take the reports of these events however they wished and assign blame as they saw fit. I hoped for the children's sake that they would. But even as I told myself these things, I knew I'd have a hard time just leaving the lodge when there was something so obviously wrong about it all. There was a part of me that had to know the truth.

Helena snapped me out of these thoughts as she said my name once more. She asked, pointedly, if I would accompany her downstairs. I wasn't sure how long I'd been off in

THE GUEST CHILDREN

173

my thoughts, but from her face it must have been longer than I'd realized.

We were the last to arrive at the table. Theresa, Simon, Agatha, and Julian were all there already. There were meagre serving platters of food on the dingy lace tablecloth between them. It seemed they'd pushed a few smaller tables together for the special occasion of a new guest.

"You two seem to be getting along," Theresa said.

I didn't like the way she said it, so I dragged my chair across the floor with a little more force than was necessary. The sound startled only Agatha, and I wished I hadn't done it. Simon drank from a pewter stein and regarded me over the lip.

"Where did you get off to today, Randall?"

"Around and about."

I looked to Agatha then, but she only smiled slightly.

"Again, you'll have to pardon the fare," Theresa said, noting that Simon and I were still eyeing each other. "What with rationing, lack of supplies . . . we do what we can."

The meal was distasteful, even to someone who'd eaten whatever scraps he could scrounge from bins in the worst of times. First, there was a plate of poached pike, the fish pale and glistening in a sauce that smelled of vinegar and mayonnaise. As the fish was served to me, I could see that the filleting job had been butchered. The fish was ragged and still full of tiny bones.

Plopped on the side of the plate next to the pike was a

small pile of long white noodles, with strands of boiled green weed and what appeared to be fried whole minnows. Although I was starving, the look and smell of the meal instantly put me off.

"We call that Littlefish Linguine," Julian said of the noodles. "It's an acquired taste, like everything else. But some have come to like it."

Simon shot Julian a look and indicated his glass on the table. "You acquired a taste for my still easily enough, didn't you."

Julian looked down at the table, chastened, and then raised a fork to his mouth. He chewed on some of the fish and everyone else ate at once, while I pushed my food around and watched them. The way they all pulled the small bones out of their mouths as they ate was grotesque, each of them ending with a little pile of them on the edge of their plate.

Simon tapped a green bottle. "Would you like to try some of my gin, Randall?"

"Thank you, no."

"Not a drinker?"

"Not on the job."

"Oh, we're on the job now, are we? Well, that's a very fine way to thank your hosts."

Her attention drawn to me now, Theresa looked down at my plate then and frowned. "Do you not like your meal?"

"It's fine." I forced down a few small bites as they

watched me eat. "I've never acquired a taste for fish, is all. Where I grew up, we mostly ate chicken and game."

"I'm sure it seems a bit funny to you, but believe me—in Italy, where we were stationed for a time before Canada, these sorts of dishes are considered a delicacy."

Working as a builder, I knew Italians. I'd worked with Italian plasterers and carpenters, and I'd seen what was in their lunch pails. It didn't look anything like this.

Helena kept glancing at me, as if she was watching to see what I noticed, to whom I was paying attention. Mostly, my attention was on our hosts, who more than anyone else had struck me as dishonest. I noticed Theresa kept glancing at Helena.

"How was your day, Helena?" she said.

"It was fine."

"I didn't see you about."

"No."

When Helena didn't elaborate, Theresa forced another smile and turned to me. "Tell us about yourself, Randall. Where were you born?"

"I was born in England. London, actually. Like the Hawksbys, and yourselves I'd imagine. My brother and I were brought over in the Home Children program, as orphans."

"Oh my," Agatha said.

"There were some troubles with that, weren't there?" Theresa asked.

"There were, yes. The family who adopted us, well,

176 Patrick Tarr

they were strict. They worked us hard. We grew up further north from here, not so far. But we left when we were young. My brother and I struggled for a while. The Depression years were tough."

"Where is your brother now?"

"In the city, we share an apartment there."

Theresa smiled. "It's nice to have family."

Though I'd shared my Edward troubles with Agatha, I didn't want to do so with Theresa and Simon, so I simply replied, "It is, yes."

"The people who adopted you, you've kept their last name?"

"It's the only name I have. Though I have no fondness for them."

Simon sighed at that. "I'm sure they did their best, and with no thanks from you."

Theresa stared at her husband. He met her cool gaze, held it briefly, then turned away and muttered something to himself. Theresa smiled an apology, and leaned closer to me. "I can't be much older than you, Randall. To think, we might have passed by one another as children in the streets of London."

"I'm not sure we'd have found ourselves in the same sorts of places. And anyway, I don't remember much of those years. Nothing at all, to tell the truth."

"Isn't it nice to have another Englishman in the house, Simon?"

"He just said he doesn't remember it."

THE GUEST CHILDREN 177

Simon meant to insult me and seemed frustrated that his words had no effect. Theresa patted his hand, which seemed to irritate him further, and he drank from his stein once more.

"Any news of the boat coming?" I asked.

"It comes when it comes," Simon said with a shrug of his hands.

"Perhaps I could walk along the shore and try to reach Lake Carver that way."

"I'm afraid not," Julian said. "It's impossible. Impassable, rather."

"And there seems to be some bad weather coming," Agatha said.

"It may be a few days yet, even a week," Theresa said. "We shall see."

Helena's hand came down then. Her fork spun into the air, sending a small arc of the fish sauce across the room before it splattered to the floor. Her sudden eruption seemed to surprise her as much as anyone.

"Please stop," she said. "No more."

Screeching back her chair, Helena rose and left, her footsteps pounding up the staircase. In the silence that followed, the house creaked in the wind, and trees rustled outside the window. I studied the faces of the people around the table. Julian and Agatha looked sad and defeated. Theresa watched the doorway as if waiting for Helena to return.

"Is she going to be all right?" I asked.

There was another moment of silence before Theresa

spoke. "She may be stuck with us, but we're stuck too, with these senseless explosions. We understand that she's mourning, but really, at some point one must learn to control oneself."

As she finished her statement, Theresa pulled a bone out of her mouth and set it down. I saw Agatha's eye flash with anger, but no one said anything. Simon refilled his stein. I got up from the table and left my food behind.

"Doesn't he know he's being used?" I heard Simon say as I went up the stairs.

Helena was down the hallway, sitting on the faded blue carpet runner. She didn't look at me as I approached, and still didn't as I sat down on the floor a few feet away from her.

"The boat won't come," she said. "It hasn't come in so long."

A knot tightened in my chest when she said that. "But why would they tell me that it would? Why would you let me believe it?"

"I hoped it was true. I always hope tomorrow will be different. With them, I couldn't say. I wouldn't like to guess what makes them do the things they do."

I reached over and tapped Helena's shoe, trying to get her to look at me. When she did, it was through hooded eyes.

"Is there something I should know?"

"No one trusts each other here. There are secrets. Our secrets are all we have. But about the children . . . Truly, I came after they'd already gone, and I don't know what happened." She waved her hand towards a floral-curtained window at the end of the hall. "It's entirely possible that they got lost out there. And I can only imagine that it was a horrible way to die. There are so many horrible ways."

"Indeed, there are."

She inched closer to me and whispered. "Will you meet me outside later? I sit on the beach by a fire at night sometimes. No one ever comes out. Will you come?"

I told her I would.

CHAPTER 24

Back in my room, I looked at the silver war medal with the frayed ribbon I'd first seen in the forest shack then found on top of my folded clothes. I thought about the footprints I'd seen in the fine layer of sand on my floor, and again on the beach. Agatha would tell me those had been a trick of the light, a breeze or a draught shifting the sand into patterns. But the medal was a thing I could hold in my hand. Maybe I'd pocketed it without meaning to after I picked it up in the shack, but I didn't think so. Someone must have left it for me.

I lay on the bed, thinking it all over, until after dark. Nothing I'd been told made sense, and I wasn't sure if there was anyone at the lodge I could trust. Growing restless, I went out into the hallway. I noticed that the door near the top of the spiral staircase was ajar. It was the room I'd figured must be Theresa and Simon's. I thought I could hear the voices of my hosts down in the kitchen and realized this might be my only chance to get a look in there. Moving as

THE GUEST CHILDREN   181

quietly as I could down the hall, I peered through the gap.
There looked to be no one inside, so I pushed the door
open and stepped over the threshold.

The room was a mess, littered with dirty clothes and
glassware. The bed was unmade, and all the curtains were
drawn, though one was parted enough to leave a wan blade
of moonlight across the carpet, bisecting a cluttered vanity.
I took a further step inside, inhaling the stale odour of
booze-sweat and old smoke I knew all too well from my
own room in the city.

Noticing that this room had a closet, whose door was
itself partly ajar, I listened again and heard sounds of clattering pots and pans in the kitchen. I'd have a moment at
least before anyone reached the top of the stairs, so I crept
across the room, mindful of creaks in the floor and the odd
overturned cup or glass. As my eyes adjusted to the darkness, I noticed photos of Simon and Theresa on the vanity,
dressed up for what I assumed were diplomatic events, both
looking proud and happy—very different from the sharp-
edged, strange people I'd come to know at Glass Point
Lodge.

I opened the closet door, cringing at the squeak it made,
but I heard no steps on the stairs. I didn't relish the thought
of getting cornered in the room with a belligerent Simon,
but I'd come this far, and I wanted to know more about my
hosts—if there was indeed anything to be found. It was dark
inside the closet, a narrow space about as long as I was tall.
First, I noticed the fine clothes hanging there—suits and

tuxedos on one side, gowns and dresses on the other—all relics of a time before the lodge and before the war. Surely a better time for them both.

At the far end, there was a shape under an old wool blanket. After I paused to listen for movement once more, I stepped into the darkness and approached it, nearly tripping on one of Simon's cast-off shoes as I went. The shape was three feet high, and it had an oddly human look under the fringed plaid blanket covering it. Making the last few steps towards whatever it was, I pulled the blanket away. When I saw what was beneath it, my hand went to my mouth and my lungs halted mid-breath. The dim light coming from behind me showed me all I cared to see.

It was a boy. Not a real boy, but an effigy of one. He was carved out of wood, hinged at his joints with loops of rusted wire. His face, with pennies for eyes, had a ghastly melted look, like the soldier from my dream. Whether this doll was made as a companion for their late son Gerald or as some tragic replacement for him didn't matter—the sight of him filled me with a sadness and a sympathy for my hosts I wouldn't have thought imaginable.

I replaced the blanket and hurried out of the closet, less concerned now about any noise I'd make and only wanting to be away from there. Crossing the room in a few hurried steps, I got to the door and peered into the hall before I went out. There was no one on the stairs, but I saw Helena at the end of the hall again, outside her room. She saw me

THE GUEST CHILDREN 183

there, frozen in place, but she said nothing. She just went back into her room and closed the door behind her.

When I went downstairs again, the dining room had been cleared and the candles blown out. I saw light through the door of the ballroom and cracked open the door to see Agatha in motion. She danced across the parquet floor in broad steps. The dance was graceful, until she hit an uneven patch, and then she'd stumble before righting herself and carrying on. I thought she might be drunk, as she laughed a little each time she faltered. It looked like she was performing for someone, but from my vantage point I couldn't see who it might be.

Easing the door shut, I went out to the screened porch. I almost missed Julian there, until I saw the flare of a pipe ember in the corner, where he was ensconced in a small chair looking out towards the lake. When he didn't acknowledge my presence, I spoke up.

"Does Agatha dance like that every night?"

"Sometimes she's too drunk."

"I thought you were in there with her."

"No, not me."

Taking the medal I'd found out of my pocket, I struck a match. Julian shielded his eyes until I asked him to look at what I had in my hand. He squinted at the medal, then his face went hard. Julian snatched for it, moving with a surprising quickness and anger.

"Where did you get that?"

"I found it inside a shack I passed in the woods. Is it yours?"

Julian looked at it, turning it over in his hands until the match burned down and I shook it out. It seemed darker than it had been before.

"I had one like it," Julian said. "I thought it was lost."

"What was it for?"

"It wasn't for anything. Just that I was there. If they'd known about the things I did, maybe they would've taken it back."

"What kind of things?"

"Count yourself lucky you never had to find out."

I thought he wouldn't continue after that, but he did. In a quiet rasp, he told me about his war, mostly talking about trench raids—blackened faces and thick rubber gloves, knuckle-dusters and spiked clubs, grenades and homemade pipe bombs thrown at sleeping enemies.

"And the prisoners," he said. He muttered something after that, but I couldn't hear it. When I asked him to repeat it, he just shook his head. I couldn't see his face anymore, but I heard the whisper of the ribbon in his hands. I'd heard stories like these before, mostly in bars, but in Julian there was no bravado. He drank some more and lit his pipe again.

I wanted to ask him about what I'd seen upstairs, but I wasn't sure whether I could trust him. He'd struck me over dinner as being somehow under Simon and Theresa's thrall.

"You said you found the medal in a shack," he said. "What shack?"

THE GUEST CHILDREN 185

"Like I said, I passed it in the woods coming from the road. I doubt I could find it again."

"What was inside?"

"Pictures and clothes. Somebody's old things. A rusty wood stove. I think someone lived there once. My brother and I lived in a place like that at one time."

"Hmm."

"Do you know who was out there?"

"It doesn't matter."

"Doesn't it? Because I was just wondering if it might have been the children."

"*Christ*, will you not shut up about them?"

The rage in his voice surprised me. He was something very different from the slow, frail, and absent old man he'd shown me so far. When he sucked on his pipe, his eyes flared red with the reflection of the ember. His cheeks puffed out and he blew smoke in my direction. If it was an attempt to intimidate me or drive me away, it was a weak one.

"I'm not sure why I should shut up about them, Julian, when nobody's told me the truth about anything since the moment I arrived."

"It's truth you want, is it?"

"That would be a start."

"The truth is, you'll be sorry you came."

Julian rose. He pointed the stump of his hand at me, and I felt the hard nub of it thumping into my chest. His breath rattled in his lungs. I heard a matching rumble of thunder in the distance, but there was no lightning yet. He shuffled past me. As he went, I felt the medal drop into my lap.

"You should have it," he said. "Since you so dearly wish to be a hero."

Julian went through the swinging door into the house. I sat there for a minute, thinking about what had just happened. He didn't like me mentioning the Hawksbys again, though he'd claimed he didn't arrive at the lodge until after they'd disappeared. I wondered what he meant by the word *hero*, what he thought he knew about me. Rising, I peered out towards the boathouse and saw a faint and flickering light. Helena, out by the bonfire as promised.

Moving outside, I stepped carefully along the path through the garden until I came to the boathouse. Passing it, I remembered the figure I'd seen inside earlier, and hurried my pace as I passed. I came to the short steps on the other side and took them down onto the small beach.

Helena sat on a log next to the struggling fire burning in the pit. She fed it some logs that looked too green and too large to burn right. Simon's handiwork chopping firewood.

When she heard my step, she looked up at me. "Simon doesn't do it properly anymore. Or stack it to dry. I do it myself sometimes, but I've been coming out here less these days."

I took a place on the log next to her, but not too close.

"I saw him. He looks like he could hurt someone with that axe."

THE GUEST CHILDREN

187

"Yes, he does."

"Are you afraid of him?"

She looked at the fire before she answered me. "It's not that he's done anything, but . . . his temper. It's frightening. He's angry about losing his boy. His only child. And because he can't change that, it makes him angry at everything."

"Gerald drowned, is that right?"

"That's what I've been told. It was long before I came here." I sat and watched the smoke curling around the new log, the flames already starting to shrink from the challenge of igniting it. Sensing someone's approach, I looked back over my shoulder towards the boathouse steps.

Helena watched me, her face half aglow from the firelight. "You heard something?"

"Not heard, I just thought someone was there."

"You feel that way a lot here."

"Agatha told me she sees things in the woods. Do you as well?"

Helena laughed, but there was no mirth in it. "Yes, we all do. It's just the isolation. Or something in the water, something in the air."

"Why did you come here, Helena?"

"I can't even remember now."

"It was after your husband died?"

"Yes. Some time after the men came to my door to tell me."

"Again, I'm sorry."

"I begged him not to go. But he had this idea that he had to fight to get our home back. He wanted to show them they were wrong, that *they* were the lesser ones, and not us. Even though some of the men he went to fight with called him the same names as they did, just in a different language. We'd got out just two weeks before the *Anschluss*, when the Germans annexed Austria. We were fortunate that we did. I understood why he'd want to fight them, of course. I hate them too. But to let that good fortune go to waste . . . I knew when he left that he'd not be so lucky a second time. After he went, I wrote and begged him to come home. Even with him dead two years, still I beg sometimes."

"Do you know how he died?"

"Sadly, yes. I do."

I looked out across the lake, and thought I saw something duck under the surface. There was no splash, but I could see the water rippling about twenty feet from shore. The fire smoked on as we sat there, some of it swirling into my eyes and blinding me as I held my breath against it. When I could see again, Helena had moved closer to me on the log.

"Would you walk out with me?"

"What do you mean?"

"Off the property, into the woods. Away from here. You came in by the trail. You're the only one who's done that. Do you think you could find your way out again?"

"I'm not sure I'd want to face that journey again. I don't even remember exactly how I ended up here. I was lost."

THE GUEST CHILDREN   189

"I can help. We can keep each other from getting lost. From seeing things. I know how it is, how to put it out of your mind."

"I don't understand what you mean."

"Yes, you do. With me along, we can get away, and find our way through to the road, and then to town, and be among the living again. You said you needed to get back."

I thought about the choices before me. Stay, and wait for a boat that might not come. God only knew what would happen to Edward in the days or weeks I'd be gone. I could try to walk along the shore. Try to put a boat together and paddle out myself, with Helena as a passenger. Or walk the woods again with her. At least a few hours to get out to the road, then the rest of the day to get to the marina, if we were lucky.

"I don't know," I said.

"Why?"

"Let's talk about it tomorrow, when it's light."

"Very well," she said. But I heard a defeat in her voice, as though she'd already decided that conversation would never happen.

She seemed to leave me then, staring off into the darkness at something I couldn't see. Maybe she was disappearing into memory in the same way I'd done before finding myself at Glass Bay. After she'd been like that a while, I spoke just to rouse her.

"I won't leave you behind, if that's what you're worried

about. However I go from here, you are welcome to come along."

She brightened then, offered her thanks, and moved over to embrace me in gratitude. It was brief, but she squeezed me tightly. After she released me, I saw another ripple on the water. I thought about what Simon said at the table about me being used.

"I'm sorry," she said.

"Don't be. But I think I'll say good night."

"Good night."

Before I left, I had to ask her something else. "Are we safe here?"

She motioned to the landscape around us. "Here, yes." She leaned forward, extending her arm, and tapped my forehead. "Here, it's harder to be sure."

It sounded like more nonsense to me, but I felt sorry for her sitting alone on the lake every night, wishing on falling stars to change things that were unchangeable, for people who were long gone to return. I didn't say anything more, just nodded and went on my way.

When I passed by the boathouse, I saw that Julian was back on the dock, staring across the dark surface of the water. He didn't have his fishing rod, but he stood in the same spot, utterly still. There was something oddly submissive about his posture. It gave the impression that he'd given up on worms and made himself the lure. I watched him until clouds passed over the sliver of moon and I couldn't see anything out there anymore.

CHAPTER 25

I couldn't sleep that night, thinking of all the strange things I'd seen, and troubling over the time I'd lost in the woods on two occasions now. There was a fierce wind up, and the draughty house felt as though it was sucking in air and wheezing it out again like an old, diseased lung. I couldn't imagine how they'd last the winter here, even with the brick fireplaces scattered about the building.

Although I'd heard everyone tromping up the stairs towards their rooms sometime after my conversation with Helena, a little after midnight I heard footfalls moving about downstairs. After they stopped, there was a new sound. At first I thought it was just the building creaking in the wind, but what started as light tapping from the lobby soon became a thumping that rattled the hanging crystals on my useless bedside lamp.

I rose, scraping a match across the side of the box to light a lantern as I shielded my eyes from the flare. Pulling on my trousers and undershirt, I crept barefoot out of my room and down the stairs. By the time I got to the bottom, the thumping had become a pounding that seemed to shake the whole lodge. I imagined every soul in the building must be awake by now, but no one else stirred. I was apprehensive of what I'd find, but I needed to see it all the same.

When I got to the bottom of the stairs, all was dark. I saw a figure standing at the far end of the front desk. The figure was kicking the plank wood base of it and then pounding the countertop with their fists, a low, whining moan escaping as they did.

It was Simon. After a few more blows he stopped his assault on the desk, wheezing. Hunched over, he looked around the corner of the front desk towards the kitchen, to a place and a person I couldn't see from where I stood.

"It's time you went away. I don't want you here anymore," he said.

"*Please don't say that.*" The reply was indistinct, a whisper from across the dark room, so faint that I couldn't be sure what was said, or even that I'd heard it at all.

Simon kicked the desk again and let out an anguished wail. "You're a liar!"

As I inched towards him, trying to get a better look at who he was speaking to around the corner, my step creaked on the floorboard. Simon finally noticed the glow of my lantern and whipped his head around to glare at me, hissing, "What do you want?"

"Who are you talking to?"

"Go back to your room. This isn't for you."

THE GUEST CHILDREN   193

I was close enough to see around the corner of the desk to where Simon was looking, but there was no one there. It was possible that Simon was as unhinged as my brother, even more so. The loss of his son, the war, the isolation. Or maybe there was something else behind it.

"Who's a liar, Simon?"

"What?"

"You called someone a liar just now."

Simon let out a sharp, bitter laugh. "Everyone here. We all are. Especially you."

"What does that mean?"

"I don't know yet, but I see it in you. Plain as day."

"I think *you're* lying about what happened to the children."

Simon crossed the lobby floor, faster than I'd have thought possible, and got one of his meaty hands around my neck before I could block his swift, lunging grasp. His eyes strained with fury as he squeezed my windpipe.

"Shut up, will you?"

I'd been in my share of fights over the years, tangling with my brother often enough on top of that. I was strong from the building work too. But Simon was uncommonly powerful in his anger. As he squeezed tighter, my vision bloomed from the loss of blood to my head. Desperate, I reached up and bent his fingers back until he howled, and then struck him in the throat as hard as I could manage with the blade of my hand.

Simon staggered back and bounced off the desk,

194 Patrick Tarr

gasping. My legs were shaking from the rush of adrenalin as I sank down, preparing for the next attack. But as Simon found his breath and growled, readying himself to rush me once more, a voice came from the stairs.

"Simon, stop it!"

Simon clenched his fists, regarding me from under his brow, his mouth open and panting. He looked feral, teeth bared like a wild animal. I could see him taking a life in this state without any trouble at all. Maybe that was how he looked after the Hawksby children did something that set him off. Michael did write in his journal that he feared the man's mood swings.

The voice from the stairs was Theresa's. She stood half-way down to the lobby in her nightgown, with a fierce look of her own that stopped us from grappling once more.

"Wake up, Simon," she said. She clapped her hands loudly three times. "Wake up now."

I looked up at her, confused, as Simon continued with his blazing glare in my direction. His shoulders heaved up and down with each breath.

"He's sleepwalking," Theresa said, turning to me. And then louder, to her husband, "You're sleepwalking, my love. Snap out of it!"

"He's been doing a lot more than walking."

"He doesn't know what he's doing."

Theresa hurried down the stairs then, her nightgown whispering against the aged parquet floor. Striding up to

THE GUEST CHILDREN   195

Simon, she put her lantern so close to his face that he finally broke his gaze away from me and shielded his eyes.

She slapped him once. "Simon, wake up!" Another slap. "Wake up!"

Simon blinked then. For a moment I feared he'd strike her, but instead he fell to his knees. I saw Agatha arrive at the top of the stairs, her mouth open. Julian came shuffling up behind her, wearing a shabby robe. He looked bleary with drink. I could see the smooth stump of his arm as he laid it on Agatha's shoulder. Whether it was to reassure her or to prevent her from speaking, I couldn't be certain.

As Theresa leaned down over Simon, he let out such a sorrowful bellow that it stopped my rolling boil of anger cold. Spittle flew from his mouth as he wailed on the floor, choking on his tears. I'd never seen a grown man cry that way. I'm not sure I'd seen anyone cry that way.

I was embarrassed to be standing there, bearing witness, so I slipped past Theresa and slunk up the stairs, brushing by Agatha and Julian without meeting their eye. They moved closer together as I passed, as if I was the one who posed a threat and not the man who'd just attacked me, nearly throttling me senseless.

Returning to my room, I stood with my back to the door for a few minutes, knowing that locking it would do little to protect me against the people who held the master key. After a while, I heard footsteps coming up the stairs once more, and some low whispers from the hosts and their guests that I couldn't make out. I wondered why Helena had never emerged from her room, as I doubted anyone could have slept through the din of my fight with Simon.

When all was quiet once more, I went back to my bed and lay down. I didn't think I'd be finding sleep that night, or for as long as I stayed at Glass Point. *I don't want you here anymore*, Simon had said. Of all of us living under the roof of that lodge, the only one I thought he could be talking about was me. Unless the living were no longer his concern.

★ ★ ★

CHAPTER 26

I'd just turned fifteen that winter on the farm when my brother finally decided to kill Mr. Sturgess. He didn't tell me what he was going to do or when he'd do it, assuring me that it was for my own good. The day it happened, I'd never have guessed it was coming. Mr. Sturgess was out chopping wood while we dutifully waited to stack it in various places outdoors and in. He would never pause in his rhythm. Grab, place, chop. We had to dart in and out to retrieve the cut logs in between quick swings of the axe. Sometimes he'd change up the rhythm and we'd have the axe come down within inches of a hand. He always laughed when that happened.

It was cold outside, snow on the ground and crystals blowing in our eyes from the wind.

As I huddled there, waiting to pounce for the next piece cut, I saw Edward watching Mr. Sturgess through narrowed eyes and muttering something to himself. Each time I dashed for the cut logs tumbling off the block, Edward edged sideways, moving around behind the man. When Mr. Sturgess raised the axe the next time, Edward struck. Just as Mr. Sturgess extended for the swing, Edward hit him in the side of the knee with a thick piece of cut wood.

Mr. Sturgess crumpled sideways, roaring in pain. As soon as he hit the ground, Edward was on him with the log, bashing him in the face with it and screeching like a wild thing trapped. He hit him three times before I could even find my voice.

"Edward, you'll kill him!"

Edward looked up at me then, confused by the statement. "I *know.*"

I told him to stop. That we had to get out of there. Mr. Sturgess wasn't dead yet. His one undamaged eye was blinking and I could still see his chest rising and falling under his heavy shirt. Edward picked up the axe and stood over Mr. Sturgess, but his gaze was on me.

"Leave him, Edward, we can run away."

"No."

"We'll hang."

"We're too young to hang."

Mr. Sturgess rolled over then. His mouth opened and closed, and he let out a sound somewhere between a yawn and a pained moan.

I crossed over to Edward, stepping over Mr. Sturgess as I did, dreading the feel of his iron grip on my ankle. When it didn't happen, I held Edward's eye and gently took the axe from him. "Let's just take what we can, and go now."

THE GUEST CHILDREN 199

We ran inside and grabbed what we could from our room, stuffing clothing and pocket knives into burlap sacks as Mrs. Sturgess shouted questions from down the stairs. When we had what we needed, we went back down. Edward had that dark look again as Mrs. Sturgess came towards us, but I said, "Mr. Sturgess hurt himself chopping wood."

"Oh, dear God . . ."

When she ran outside to see what had happened, we took some cans of food, a loaf of bread, and a bottle of milk in our sacks and went for the door. On his way out, Edward smashed the three china figures Mrs. Sturgess kept on the mantel, which she'd had since she was a little girl. I heard her shouting outside. I grabbed Edward and we ran out into the dark and cold.

We started walking through the forest. We figured it was smart not to go to Bristow, because that's where they'd look for us first. We went in the opposite direction, braving the longer trek towards a further-off town, thinking that by the time they looked there, we'd already be long gone.

Even in the extra clothes we'd put on, we were freezing before long. I might've turned back if I hadn't known just how bad it would be for us if we did. We trudged on through the snow, feeling it gather in the tops of our boots until our ankles were as numb as our faces. At least we had some woollen mitts to keep our hands from falling off. Edward didn't say a word the whole time, even as I asked him where we could go and what we could do.

Once we got to the town, after five hours of snow and the naked undergrowth that shredded our cold-red cheeks, we didn't want to linger. It was morning now, but few people were out and about yet. We had to be careful, and I watched the road for any sign of the Sturgess truck as we thought about what we could do to get further away.

When an elderly woman came out of the general store, we made up a story about a sick father and begged a ride from her. I made Edward let me do the talking. Where she dropped us wasn't a long way off, but at least it got us further away from the farm. We made it to one town, then the next. Sometimes working for coins, sometimes begging, sometimes stealing. A lot of the time, we were hungry. We skimmed trash bins for food, but there was rarely anything to find.

Out in the world, we weren't big enough to defend ourselves, and we often suffered for it. We found some good places to hole up, abandoned buildings or other hidden lairs where we'd be alone, and safe. But during that time, everyone was suffering, and some people liked to pass their suffering along. Edward and I looked after each other. And there was a part of us that was always looking over our shoulders, expecting to see Sturgess coming for us with his axe raised high.

We never knew what became of Mr. and Mrs. Sturgess. Edward used to talk about going back to the farm to finish the job. I always laughed, like it was a joke. But I knew that it wasn't. He could still be kind and innocent sometimes,

THE GUEST CHILDREN 201

but the streak of darkness was never far off. Every bad encounter with a stranger added to his list of those from whom he wanted vengeance.

I relived those lost days in my dreams that night in the lodge. Some of the events were combined or changed somehow, but always some version of things that really happened to us. But then, after a time, the dreams shifted, and it was something else entirely.

I found myself at home in the city in our room. Edward was there. We weren't boys anymore, but the men who'd said goodbye to each other days before. I had an unsettled feeling and looked to my brother for guidance, something I was not prone to do in ordinary times.

"Why are we here?" I said.

"We live here, Randall."

"Are you okay? I've been worried."

"You shouldn't have let it happen."

"What?"

"You shouldn't have left me in this place alone."

"I had to. You're safest here at home."

"This isn't our home, Rand. It just looks like it."

Edward went to the kitchen table. He looked at me gravely and then poked the table with an outstretched finger. When his finger made contact, the table dissolved into a million grains of sand, streaming away into a pile on the floor with that darkly jingling sound. When it was done, Edward put the same finger to his lips. Even if he hadn't, I was speechless.

Hearing a step behind me, I saw two children I knew were Michael and Frances Hawksby in the tiny flat with us, looking up at me. Their eyes were wide and white. I thought I could see movement inside their pupils, like swirls of sand. I put my finger to my lips, as Edward had for me. The children followed suit. When their fingers touched their lips, their faces began to fall away. Soon they were just two shocked mouths on blank edifices of shifting sand.

I ran to the door to escape from the sight of them, but when I touched the handle, the door too disintegrated before me, revealing a darkness on the other side so complete that the sight of it sucked the breath from my lungs. I'm not sure where it was in the nightmares that followed that I knew for certain I was dreaming, but at some point my awareness inserted itself into the succession of horrifying visions, and I screamed at myself to wake up.

Somehow, I managed it. I was rigid as a plank and lying on my back on the sagging cot in my lodge quarters. I wiped sweat from my face with one hand, while the other remained dangling over the side of the bed. There was such a panic in me that I struggled to remember how to breathe. I was surprised that I'd managed to fall asleep after everything that had happened that night, and it all started running through my mind once more.

Until something brushed against my hand from under the bed frame.

The last vestiges of sleep blew away and my eyes opened

to regard the ceiling above me. I felt something touch me again. Before I could yank my hand up and onto the safety of the bed, a cold hand squeezed mine so tightly that I felt the bones creak.

Leaping out of the bed, I skidded across the floor and lost my balance, tumbling through the small room and crashing against the door. It was still dark out, with just the veiled light of a crescent moon coming through the curtains. I couldn't see anything in the shadows under the mattress, but I knew there was something down there.

Getting down low, I peered into the darkness. I shouted when I saw two eyes peering back at me. They looked just like what I'd seen blinking from deep in the stone crevasse in the woods. It took everything I had to fight the urge to scream once more.

I buried the fear in my voice when I spoke. "Whoever you are, come out."

A shadow skittered out from under the bed and rushed at me. As I dove to the side, I saw that it wasn't me the figure was going for—it was the door. As I sat crumpled on the floor in my shorts, I saw who fled the room, leaving the door yawning open into the dark hall beyond.

There was a fine layer of sand on the floor again, and I could see the footprints she left as she raced through it. I didn't see her face, but I saw her filthy dress and her long brown hair. She didn't look at me. I think she was as frightened in that moment as I was. It took a moment for me to pull myself together and get some more clothes on, but then

I followed her out the door and down the hall. I heard the rattle of the door off the screened porch as it flapped shut.

I passed through the lobby, past the place where Simon tried to throttle me, and saw an unfinished glass of liquor left behind on the front desk. The temptation to knock it back before whatever I would face next was strong, but I thought if I stopped moving, I'd never be able to start again. Passing through the porch, I went out the door and eased it shut behind me. I looked through the garden and down towards the lake, and then I saw it.

The door to the boathouse was open.

It was pitch-dark in there, of course, but I thought I saw a shift in the shadows beyond the reach of the moonlight. I went up to the entrance and stood there. A hush fell over the woods, and the sudden silence unnerved me.

"Hello . . ." I said. "You were in my room just now."

At first, I heard only something like that long, hollow hiss I'd heard in my dreams, but then a small voice replied, "It was *our* room before it was yours."

"I didn't know that."

"Well, it was. But they took our things out and hid them away."

"I found them," I said. "I found the pages that Michael wrote too. Can you please show yourself? I promise I won't hurt you. I came here to find you. I was told you were gone."

Silence stretched out, as I tried to make sense of the darkness inside the boat house. The lake water lapped against the sides, and once again I thought I saw movement.

"We'd rather you came in here. We promise we won't hurt you either."

The way she said it gave me pause. It hadn't even occurred to me that could be possible. "Is Michael in there with you too, Frances?"

"How do you know our names?"

She sounded angry then. I looked back to the house, but all was dark. There were no faces watching me from the upstairs windows, though I wished there were so I could call out. I wanted someone to witness whatever was about to happen. Even Simon's company might've been welcome. I thought about going in to rouse Helena, but instead I stepped inside.

"My name is Randall Sturgess. I know your names because your family sent me here to find you. They're quite concerned, you know."

"That's not why you're really here," she said.

"Why would you say that?"

"Because it's true."

"Come closer, please. Don't you want to go home now?"

Two shadows approached me. It was a tremendous thing to have found the children, seemingly unharmed. When they got close, I could see their pale faces. They would be in their teens now, around the same age as Edward and me when we ran away. They looked every bit as scared and lost as I was at that time. They were terribly skinny and dirty, in tattered layers of clothing. I knew then for certain it was them I'd seen standing on the ridge at Glass Bay. There was no question about it. Though I'd never seen even a photo of them before, they looked just as they had in my dream of Edward of moments before, only older.

They looked up at me, eyes shining in what little light was coming through the entryway. They were so still for a moment that they looked like oversized dolls on display in the window of a children's shop, or the sad wooden thing I'd found in the closet.

"We can't leave," she said. "And neither can you."

PART 4

LOST ONES

CHAPTER 27

"You were the one we saw at Glass Bay," Frances said. "Did you find our notes?"

"Yes. And I saw you there, but . . ."

"You thought it was a dream."

"Where have you two been all this time? They told me you ran away."

"We've been here."

"Do they know this, your aunt and uncle?"

Michael spoke now. "They've seen us. But they act like they haven't."

The siblings' voices were eerily similar, as if it was the same quiet English child speaking through different bodies.

"Was it you who left me the medal?"

Frances shook her head. "It was Michael. He put it in your room, so you'd know we were here. We took it from the old man."

"But how have you survived all this time?"

"We built shelters," Frances said. "You saw one of our

shacks. When it gets too cold, we sneak into parts of the lodge where they don't look. We can get around without them seeing. We take food sometimes, when we can't catch or pick anything, but they don't have much anymore. Some of them know about us, but they think we're dead."

"We're *not* dead." Michael stomped his foot as he said it, hard enough to rattle the old tools hung on the walls of the boathouse. I took a step back from his anger. Although he was still a boy, and slight of frame, something about him made me uneasy.

Frances put a hand on her brother's arm to calm him. I'd done the same to Edward more than once when he started teetering into rage.

"You're saying they knew where you were all this time, but they didn't help you?"

"They're afraid." I saw a glint off Michael's teeth when he spoke.

"Did Simon do something to you? Did he hurt you?"

Frances sighed, as if already growing tired of explaining things to me. "Simon only cares about Gerald. He's always talking to him. When we found out about it, he was going to hurt us."

"Found out about what?"

"About what happened to Gerald."

"Gerald didn't drown?"

A soft sigh escaped from Michael. "Not the way you mean it, no. He didn't drown."

THE GUEST CHILDREN 211

The children were so peculiar, but if their story about living in the woods was true, that was no surprise. When my brother and I were still boys, and living rough, we developed strange behaviours, tics, and manners of speaking, as if girding ourselves in a secret, shared armour against the world. With no one to measure themselves against, two alone can become even stranger than one.

"Listen, Frances, Michael . . . you're safe now."

Now Frances laughed, but it was short and sharp and devoid of mirth. The lake water lapped against the boathouse pilings, as if in echo of her.

"I can protect you. We're going to go inside and confront your aunt and uncle about what they've told me. And then I'm going to take you away from here."

"*No*," Michael said. It was somehow both a plea and a warning.

"They can't know we've spoken with you," Frances said.

"Why not?"

"They don't want other people to know about everything. They can't let you tell people what happens here. They might do something."

"Don't you want me to help you?" I said. "I'm not afraid of Simon. If I show the others that I've found you—"

Frances shook her head. "You can't trust the others. They don't want to leave, no matter what they tell you. Even though they're sick from being here, they're afraid to go."

212 Patrick Tarr

"What is it you want me to do, then? I'm not leaving without you."

"You won't leave," Michael said.

"Nobody is going to stop us—"

"You don't know!"

Michael's shout rang in my ears as he rushed out of the boathouse, his feet clapping across the planks. After a moment the sound stopped abruptly, as if he'd simply vanished, but I realized he must have leapt from the walkway into the sand next to it. Frances gazed at me in the dark, a wet shine in her eyes. She sniffed and wiped at her nose, and instinctively I searched for Agatha's handkerchief, but I'd left it in my room.

"Is your brother all right?"

"I tried to look after him. But I did a poor job."

She sounded mature beyond her years, worn down and defeated. I leaned down closer to her, trying to establish some rapport. I needed her to convince her brother to trust me. I imagined if I brought the children back to the lawyer's office with me, there might be a happy ending for all of us. A trip back home for them, and a bonus for me.

"I have a younger brother too. I look after him most of the time. It's hard."

"Why aren't you looking after him now?"

"I've been trying to. I need to get back home to him. I will leave here, you see. I have to, and you need to convince your brother to come."

I looked around the boathouse, the shadows resolving

THE GUEST CHILDREN   213

into the shapes of things. A breeze came in through the opening and hit me with the dank, sulphurous smell of the lake. Moving along the creaky boards to the door, I looked out for Michael but didn't see him anywhere. Still shaking off sleep, I wasn't entirely convinced that this wasn't a dream. But I could still feel Frances's cold hand gripping mine from underneath the bed.

Turning back to her, I said, "No more fooling around. Come back into the house with me. I'm not afraid—"

"Stop saying that when you are."

"Please, Frances. Do as you're told."

"No."

"I don't understand. Don't you want to go home?"

"If you're going to take us away, you can't tell them about it. That's the only way it can work. It has to be our secret."

"Frances, that's enough, just come along now—"

When I reached out for her, Frances struck me with both hands, pushing my chest with a force beyond her size. I staggered back into the side of the boathouse, nets and oars rattling behind me as I smacked my head. Something crashed to the deck boards.

I heard thumping footsteps. By the time my vision cleared, Frances was gone. When I went out to look for her and her brother, they were nowhere. Not in the garden, on the dock, or on the beach. I called out to them in a low voice.

"Michael, Frances . . . ?"

There was no answer.

But I did see someone else. Standing out on the surface of the lake, the figure was too far off to make out, but they were there—impossibly perched on the dark water just as I'd been in my dream with Edward the day before.

It looked to me like they raised a hand in greeting.

All else faded away until I could hear only my heartbeat and that empty drain sound. Again, I felt as if the cold breath of a giant lung was pushing and pulling the air around me. I took a step towards the shore for a closer look, despite a swirling unease that almost made me sick. As I did, something gripped my arm so hard I felt the tissue pushing into bone. I tried to pull the arm back, but I couldn't break free. I looked down to see Michael gripping onto me.

"Come and find us in the morning. We'll meet you at Glass Bay. At the Sand Palace."

I yanked my arm back and Michael let go. The figure was gone now, but I could still feel it there, still feel its pulse thrumming in the water and in the earth under my feet. I was troubled by what I'd seen but didn't want to lose my chance with Michael.

"You'll come with me, you and Frances?"

"We'll have to be clever. You will, I mean. To get away. You'll have to make it safe to take us out."

"How can I do that?"

"You might have to kill them all."

After he said it, Michael ran away into the forest,

although I called out for him to come back. It haunted me how much he'd reminded me of my brother with those final words. I stood there, trying to make sense of what I'd seen and heard, but there was no sense to be made. I was tired of the games and the lies, the odd pronouncements, and even my own dreams. Leaving the boathouse, I strode up through the garden and into the lodge, where I slammed the door with as much force as I could behind me.

Knowing from Simon's pounding earlier that night that noise travelled well in the building, I took up the dinner bell and shook it at the end of my arm, the clapper striking the bell so hard and fast that it barely had time to resonate. When I heard the first step from upstairs, I stopped shaking. The bell's final note held and rang through the house. I could feel the vibrations in my clenched teeth, feel it buzzing through the walls and the glass in the picture frames.

One by one, they came down. First Julian, blinking and unsteady in flannel pyjamas. Then Agatha, who seemed alert and awake already, fully dressed despite it being the middle of the night. Helena, on the other hand, was hollow-eyed and looked like she'd been pulled out of a fitful slumber. She wore a nightgown, seafoam with gold trim, that looked expensive.

Theresa and Simon came last. Theresa led the way, and her sharp eyes found me immediately, with a look that felt like both a threat and a question. Simon was shirtless, bleary-eyed, and drunk, his hand gripping the railing as it came down just as it had gripped my throat a few hours before. I could feel the bruises forming there already, as I could on my arm from Michael. Simon paused near the bottom step, looking sick and confused, before Theresa noticed him lagging and grabbed his hand, pulling him to her like a frustrated mother would an unruly child.

"What is it *now*?" Theresa said. As if I was the one who'd been kicking the front desk earlier. As if I was the one who'd lost two children for years and seemed to be keeping her guests as prisoners here.

"I saw Michael and Frances tonight," I told them.

Each of the gathered had a different reaction to those words, but not one of them looked surprised. Theresa laughed. Simon looked like he'd be sick. Agatha sighed. Julian looked angry, and I could almost imagine his phantom hand clenching into a fist. Helena looked away.

I felt them all ease closer, as if surrounding me to prevent my escape. They put me in mind of scavenger birds, and I didn't like the feeling of them ringing me in.

"Could someone explain to me how that's possible?"

Theresa spoke first, as her husband swayed on his feet. "It's *not* possible."

"I just spoke to them now."

"Randall, you had a terrible time getting here. A harrowing journey. When we found you, you were distraught, saying all sorts of mad things. Not only that, you had an unfortunate quarrel with my husband just a few hours ago. I think you're in a rather agitated state of mind, and that the darkness and the isolation up here can put one rather out of sorts even at the best of times—"

"I'm not *out of sorts.*"

"If you say so," Simon whispered.

Glaring at him, Theresa continued, "I feel the need to ask, Randall, have you ever seen a doctor about neuroses or mental disorders?"

"We've all heard you screaming in your sleep, old chap," Julian said.

"I do no such thing."

I looked to Helena, expecting her support, but she cast her eyes to the floor. Whether it was because Julian was right or because she didn't want to get involved, I couldn't be sure. To see them all denying such an obvious truth sparked a rage in me that I struggled to tamp down. Before I could say more, Agatha beat me to it.

"I saw him watching the lodge from the tree line earlier tonight," she said, pointing to me. I felt betrayed by her after our long talk in the afternoon, though I had no reason to expect her loyalty. "He stood there for hours, just looking into the windows."

"That's impossible," I said. I don't know what I'd been expecting when I came in, but I'd never have believed it could all get turned around on me so quickly. The ring of them around me felt like it was tightening, though I hadn't seen any of them move closer.

"Tell us, Randall . . . the children, what did they look like?" Theresa asked.

"Frances . . . she was in a shabby brown dress with a blue jacket and a shawl over her shoulders . . . And Michael, an oversized jacket with the trousers cut short."

"And you saw them where?"

"First Frances was in my room. Then they were both outside, in the boathouse."

Simon spoke up then, scoffing. "It's pitch-dark in there. You couldn't see your hand in front of your face."

Theresa frowned. "And how would a girl of that age fit under a bed so small?"

"I don't know, but she was there. She touched my hand."

"You're telling us you've seen a ghost," Theresa said. "Two ghosts."

"Of course not. I just told you, she touched me."

Theresa looked sorry for me then. "But the children are gone, Randall. We've told you so many times. They're gone."

Simon spoke up again, bolstered now, the two of them descending upon me as one. "What else have you seen out there? Pink elephants and unicorns?"

"Who were you talking to in the lobby, Simon? I heard you, before you attacked me. The children told me you speak to Gerald. They said something bad happened to him, that he didn't really drown. Maybe someone could explain what they meant by that."

Theresa gasped and crossed the room in two long strides to slap me across the face. The force of it turned my head sideways, and my cheek went numb before the flare of pain

THE GUEST CHILDREN 219

hit. It was the second act of violence from these two in a matter of hours.

"Don't you dare speak of him."

Helena came forward then, blocking Simon's path as he stepped towards me. "Randall," she said. "Please listen . . ."

"*Yes*, Helena," I answered, keeping my eyes firmly on Simon. I could see his fist flexing at his hip.

"I think you need to come outside for a moment."

"I don't see why I should."

A trip outdoors wasn't what I needed, not at all, but when Helena came over and gently took me by the hand, I let her lead me out the back door. Once we were outside and a good distance from the lodge, we stood under the shrouded night sky with the forest watching us from a hundred yards away. I instinctively looked to the tree line, remembering Agatha's words, as if I'd see myself there, watching me back. The silence seemed to have taken physical form in a wispy nighttime fog slithering through the trees. I longed for the dawn to come.

Helena still had her hand on my arm when she leaned in close. She held me in the same place where Michael had gripped so tightly, and it was still sore. But the warmth of her body and the feeling of her words in my ear calmed me, until all that remained of the conflict inside the lodge was a swirling sense of confusion.

"It must be a secret, Randall. You must tell them that you were mistaken." She was close enough that I could feel her breathing. "If they think you'll tell others the things you've seen here, they'll never let us leave."

"That's what the children said. But I don't need permission. Michael and Frances have a family to go back to, and so do I. They can't stop us."

"Think about how hard it was to get here, how quickly you got lost. Imagine doing that with Simon chasing after you. He knows the woods, and—"

"And what? What has he done?"

"Pretend you had a nightmare. We all have them here. Tell them you had one about the children. That you were in a state when you woke up. And then go back to bed. When you're certain the others are asleep, come to my room. I'll do my best to explain everything. I wanted to tell you before, but . . ."

Breaking away from me before I could respond, she went back into the lobby where the others were still waiting. I followed, flustered and confused. The others ringed us in the lobby when we returned, four expectant and anxious faces wondering what I'd do next. Again, I had a disturbing sense that they were more interested in devouring me than hearing me speak. Helena put a hand on my shoulder as if she were making introductions.

"Randall's calmed down now. He's realized he just had a nightmare about the children."

I looked at Simon and Theresa, both studying me with narrowed eyes.

"That's not what he said a moment ago," Simon said.

THE GUEST CHILDREN   221

"I guess it makes sense now," I said. My voice didn't sound like my own. "I had a bad dream about Michael and Frances, and I found myself outside. It's just that it seemed so real. I'm afraid I suffer the same affliction as Simon, walking in my sleep. And, as Theresa said, your mind can play tricks in such an isolated spot. I was just in a bit of a state, I'm afraid."

"Well, of course that makes sense," Theresa said. "Let's all just get back to bed, shall we? Tomorrow is another day."

"Thanks for your understanding," I said. "I just need some rest."

And that was that. Without another word, the four of them shuffled up the stairs to their rooms. All it took was for me to deny what I'd seen with my own eyes. Helena stood before me, arms crossed in front of her. I realized I was shaking, and I tried to still myself. When Theresa looked back at us, Helena followed her up the stairs as if she'd been summoned.

I stood in the lobby, listening to the house creak.

★ ★ ★

CHAPTER 28

Back in my room again, I looked out the window towards the boathouse and the night water behind it. I didn't believe that I'd simply had a nightmare and walked out there in some dream state, following a long-dead girl summoned from my imagination. Nor did I think the others believed that, no matter what they said. Not from the way they looked at me.

But if I was entertaining all possibilities, I had to consider through the events of the past two days that I'd begun to share some of my brother's instabilities. The way the Masts and their residents treated me did seem in line with the way strangers might react to an unbalanced and unpredictable guest. I had to at least entertain the notion that what was truly behind all the strange things I'd seen and heard at Glass Point Lodge was the imminent collapse of my own mind. These afflictions did run in families, after all. Edward and I didn't know our real parents, but maybe they suffered from such delusions too, the only inheritance they left us.

THE GUEST CHILDREN 223

Helena seemed to believe me, and she seemed to know things. But the strange accusation from Agatha, that she'd seen me watching the lodge from the tree line, was the one thing I couldn't shake. It roamed through my thoughts, searching for a place where it made sense.

Maybe Agatha truly had seen me there, in the same fugue state that had spirited me down to Glass Bay on two occasions already. Maybe all their talk of the dangers of my surroundings was meant to protect me, not themselves. It seemed I couldn't take my own word for my movements around the resort anymore. That frightened me as much as anything else I'd seen, or even dreamed.

The other two possibilities I needed to consider were that Agatha was lying about what she saw, or that the person she'd seen out her window wasn't me at all. I'd sensed a presence in the boathouse, and I didn't believe it was one of the children. I'd seen the figure out on the lake as well, and glimpsed someone in the trees in my search for the lodge. There could be someone else out there. Who, I couldn't imagine. But it was one explanation, however implausible.

That Agatha was lying was the most likely answer. But it raised a new question. *Why?* As I turned away from my window, I wondered when I should go see Helena again, what new strangeness she'd have to share. She seemed to be my only ally, but there was something strange about her, and it was more than just her vague manner of speaking. I decided to wait a little longer, until the others had gone back to sleep. I lay in my bed to pass the time, remembering the cold grasp of that hand from below.

I don't remember falling asleep again, but I woke to a thunderous boom. It shook the house and rained tinkling sand down from the rafters. It startled me so much that I leapt out of bed, lost my balance, and careened into the wardrobe, gripping it to steady myself. For a moment there was a stillness and a silence that felt like the end of all things. A tremor started up in my legs, and I had to hang on to the wardrobe to keep from going down.

Overwhelmed by the sudden assault on my senses, I vomited onto the floor. What came out of me was sand, stained red with blood and stinking of rot and gasoline. More and more came out, until it became clear to me that my body wasn't made of bone, flesh, and sinew at all, but only this slick, corrupted sand.

When I felt as if I'd thrown up all that I was, I woke. I was still in my bed, and I knew instantly that I wasn't alone. Sweat-slick and panting, I saw a form sitting on the bed next to me. The man was hunched over and shirtless, wheezing softly, and I could see beaded sweat on his skin. From the size of him, I knew it could only be Simon.

"You get used to the dreams," he said. He lifted his right hand and made a fluttering motion, just like Agatha had out in the woods.

"Get out of my room."

"I thought you wanted to know things."

THE GUEST CHILDREN   225

He turned to me, and I could see he'd been crying. His unshaven face was puffy from the homemade gin, and I saw that his bare shins under his shorts were covered in bruises and abrasions. Following my gaze, he shrugged.

"The trails are uneven when you've had too much to drink."

I sat up and shifted closer to the wall, away from him. "You have something to tell me, Simon?"

"You've been to the Sand Palace, you said."

"Yes."

"I built it for Gerald. After he died. He'd always begged me for a playhouse. He was lonely here. But I didn't have the time for it. After he died, I did. I needed something to do. I tried to make it look just like the lodge, but I buggered it up." He held out his broad palms in front of him then, and turned to show them to me. "I've never been good with my hands."

"Why are you telling me this?"

"I was the only one who ever went inside. I spent weeks in there. I begged and begged for my boy to come back and play with me." Simon started to cry again, a silent, pulsing shudder that creaked the bedsprings.

"What happened to Gerald?"

"I don't know. I don't. We found him on the beach."

"You told me before that he'd drowned."

"Yes. In a manner of speaking."

"What does that mean?"

"His mouth was full of sand." Simon's voice broke

when he said it. I got that cold, slithering feeling in my belly again, the one that started right after I arrived at the lodge.

"How could that be?"

"I don't know."

"Do you think someone killed him?"

"Yes."

"Was it you, Simon?"

He spun on me then, pinning me to the bed. I struggled, but he had all his weight bearing down on me and I couldn't break free. His red, unshaven face came down close to mine, and I could smell the liquor on his breath.

"Don't you fucking say that," he said.

After he spoke, his rage wavered for the briefest of moments. I threw all my strength up and sideways, barely managing to heave him off me and onto the floor. Simon got up on his hands and knees, drool coming out of his mouth, and threw up on the floor. It was the exact spot where I'd done it in my dream.

Without another word, Simon got up and went to the door. He looked at me before he went out again, but I couldn't read a thing in the look. I swore and sat there in the dark, hands clutching the sweat-damp sheets as I waited for him to return. He didn't.

A few minutes later, I was standing outside Helena's door with the sharp copper tang of blood in my mouth, likely from biting my tongue in my struggle with Simon.

THE GUEST CHILDREN 227

Before I knocked, I heard whispering coming from the other side of the door.

Helena's voice, certainly, and then someone else's. It was a man, which meant Simon or Julian. I didn't relish encountering Simon again so soon, but before I could hear what was being said, Helena opened the door. She looked me up and down and I saw her eyes widen.

"Who are you talking to?" I said.

She shook her head, a finger to her lips. I moved past her into the room and looked around, but there was no one there. Helena's arms were tight around her sides, and I thought I must be scaring her. It was dark in her room, but it was obvious she hadn't been sleeping.

"There's no one here, Randall."

"But I heard you talking."

"Yes."

My breath was coming fast and the taste of blood in my mouth was overpowering. "Did you not hear all that in my room just now?"

"I heard nothing."

"The struggling, the raised voices, none of it?"

"No."

"I don't understand what's happening."

I heard the creak of floorboards in the next room. Helena trod lightly over to me and whispered, "Come with me. Walk softly."

We tiptoed down to the cluttered and reeking kitchen, away from prying eyes and ears. Helena brought a lantern, and the flickering shadows it threw off the wood stove and icebox looked monstrous. I only noticed then that I was shaking.

"Randall, tell me what happened when you saw the children."

I told her about waking from a nightmare to find Frances under my bed, grasping my hand. About following her down to the boathouse, where I saw Michael, and all that they said while we were in there. I realized that I was doing what the children told me *not* to do, telling Helena about them, but I had to say it out loud. And I felt, rightly or wrongly, that Helena might be able to help me. When I finished telling her everything, I was sweating. I wiped my forehead with my bare arm before Helena passed me a tea towel.

"I've never seen them," she said. "I've thought I have sometimes, here and there just outside my view. But there are so many of them here, I'm never sure what's real."

"So many of what?"

"It's going to be hard for you to believe. It's not like anything else. Nothing else you've ever encountered. There is something about this place, about Glass Bay. It lets you see people . . . People who are gone. It shows you your lost ones. But of course, it's not really them."

"You're speaking of ghosts."

"No, not ghosts."

"Then what?"

THE GUEST CHILDREN 229

"I don't know . . . They're more like our memories and feelings, made real. But they are tainted, these things. They are sometimes very frightening."

"Even if I believed that, why would you stay here?"

"It was better than nothing." She pressed a hand to her chest, thumped her breastbone. "That's why we stay, all of us. But what we must always remember is that our dead ones are bait, and this place is the trap."

Although what she said made no sense, there was something in her words that felt right. I felt the truth in them shimmering through me, like that feeling in my bones when I'd rung the bell in the lobby.

"Randall . . . you've seen people since you've been here, yes? People in the woods or in the water. I know that you have."

I nodded, not wanting to speak what I'd seen out loud for fear that something would appear in the kitchen behind her.

"I've seen a boy. I've seen a woman with red hair."

"And a soldier?"

"In my dreams, maybe. I'm not sure."

"Nevertheless, he's been out there. With the others."

I realized that the soldier must have been who she was talking to when I stood outside her room. Her late husband. Of course.

"I'm going to ask you to be calm now, Randall."

"I *am* calm."

"You are not. You're breathing quickly, you're sweating,

and your eyes are very wide. But I'm going to ask you to turn around. And when you do, you're going to see someone standing there. Please don't shout. We are safe."

I didn't know what to say, but I knew I didn't want to turn around. As if sensing I wouldn't do it, Helena put her hands on my shoulders, turning me to face a dark corner of the kitchen. Impulsively, I jolted backwards when I saw what was there.

"No," I said.

As if that would change anything.

It was a man in a bloodstained and tattered US Army uniform. He wore a gas mask, those round glass-disc eyes glittering in the light from the lantern. He didn't react to me as I did to him. He stood there, still and impassive as a waxwork effigy. My quick breaths whistled in my lungs as I looked at him. It was the only sound in the tiled room. Helena shushed me, squeezing my shoulders tighter.

"Randall, this is my husband."

"Your husband is dead."

"Yes."

"So what . . . is that."

"I think what it is . . . is my memory of him. Mixed up with my grief for him, and what I know about . . . what happened to him. He was killed in an explosion, you see. His face was torn away, and that is the man who visits me here."

The soldier moved for the first time, putting a damaged hand to his chest. It was a slow, gentle motion, but I felt every nerve in my body scream at the wrongness of it.

THE GUEST CHILDREN   231

"He won't hurt you. He will only try to make you follow him to the bay, which you must never do. It comes from there, whatever it is. It started with Gerald."

"Simon told me that Gerald was murdered."

"Did he."

I forced myself to look away from the man in the gas mask. "What do you know about what happened to him?"

"Nothing. It was before my time here. I know now that if I stay here any longer, I'll go mad. Leaving means the end of . . . him. I wasn't ready for that before. But I think I am now. I need to leave while I'm still able."

"You don't know why this is happening."

"Theresa and Simon, as much as they'll speak of it, don't seem to know either. They started seeing Gerald again some weeks after he died. I don't know what happened to that boy. I only know that Simon built that house for him after he was gone. Perhaps in those long nights of grief, something was conjured out of the dark. Or perhaps there's just something in this place that seeks out the broken people, the ones with holes in them that it can fill. But they're under a spell, both of them. Theresa and Simon believe that spectre is really their son. They told the man with the boat to stop coming. They don't want others to know what goes on here, because they fear if they do . . . it will stop."

"Why did you ever come here?"

"I don't remember why, and that's the truth. I was in Toronto. My parents moved there from New York. They left Europe before us and helped us come over."

She gestured to her husband, still watching me from behind the gas mask. It was as if I'd forgotten he was there. Seeing him again shocked me nearly as much as the first time.

"I was staying with them. It was sometime after I got the news. One day, I just bought a ticket for the train and I came here. It was as if I was called."

"How long ago?"

"A year, more or less, I think. Why did *you* come?"

"I was hired to find the children."

"By whom? Do you remember his name?"

I didn't remember. All I could recall was finding the newspaper clipping in the trash, visiting a silver-haired man in a wood-panelled office who told me about Frances and Michael. It couldn't be possible that I'd imagined it all, and yet when I looked back, my memory of meeting that agent of the Hawksby family felt as abstract as my visits to the battle-scarred beach of my dreams.

"Randall, I think you were called here, like the rest of us."

I couldn't make sense of what she was saying. And I couldn't look away from her husband now. His eyes weren't visible through the lenses in the bloodied gas mask he wore, but I felt his gaze on me as intensely as I'd felt Simon's hand around my neck earlier that night.

"You haven't told me his name," I said.

Helena looked surprised that I'd mentioned it. I could see her choosing whether she should lie to me, but I couldn't discern which choice she made.

THE GUEST CHILDREN 233

"Emil," she said. "His name is Emil."

At the sound of his name, the soldier cocked his head and took a step forward.

"That's okay," Helena said.

He came up and stood before me, and I could see the lantern flame reflected in the lenses as the light flickered across his stained uniform. I felt his presence there in front of me. He had substance, not like what I imagined a ghost to be like at all, but still he said nothing.

"You were speaking to him," I said. "I heard you."

"He won't speak when others are around. Only to me."

I looked down to see that Emil held out a ghastly pale and wounded hand. There was a ragged hole through the palm. I could see the dingy floor tiles through it. Revolted by the sight, I stepped back. Emil lowered his head. I'm not sure how I could sense the weight of his sadness in the absence of a face, but there was such a feeling of despair in that empty kitchen that even the lantern light seemed to dim.

Needing to get out of there, I backed towards the door. I moved away from the pool of light and the sight of Emil. As I did, Helena went to him. She put her arms around him and patted him on the top of the mask. He bowed his head, but kept watching me. Helena watched me backing away too, soothing her dead husband. I couldn't tell if the look she was giving me was disappointment or absolution, and I didn't care.

★ ★ ★

CHAPTER 29

When I fled the kitchen, I hoped it would finally be growing light outside, but Glass Point was still in full darkness. The moon, wherever it was, was cloaked behind a mass of dark clouds rolling in over the landscape. I couldn't make the trip to Glass Bay to find Michael and Frances until there was some daylight, not after what had happened to me out there on my previous journeys. It seemed impossible for the night to stretch on for so long, and with so many unsettling turns. It felt as if some cruel and potent force was holding off the dawn.

I found myself in the dark expanse of the ballroom, trying to make sense of what I'd just seen and heard. I wondered where the children were right then, what horrors they'd witnessed in all the long nights they'd spent living around the lodge. The strange entries I'd come upon in Michael's journal made sense now—so much sense that I almost didn't want to think about it.

Instead, I thought of Edward, imagining the storms of

THE GUEST CHILDREN 235

fear and resentment he'd have stirred up in himself by now.
Yes, there was a part of me that wanted to stay gone. I couldn't
imagine what would become of my brother if I simply never
returned, but so many times in recent years, especially after
things ended with Mildred, I'd imagined a different life
for myself. A life that wasn't tethered to someone who held
me back from dreams of better times and better places, but
kept me rooted in a shared past I wanted to leave behind.

Hearing movement and voices in the kitchen then, I
couldn't bear the thought of Helena and Emil coming into
the ballroom to find me. Creeping across the uneven floor,
I went to the cloakroom before anyone emerged, and ducked
inside.

It took me a moment in the dark, but I soon found the
matchbook and candle I'd used before and shed some light
on the space. The suitcases belonging to Frances and
Michael were gone. So were the hanging coats from the
rack. And when I stuck my hand in the hole in the wall
where I'd found the journal entries, everything in there
was gone too. Maybe the children had come for them,
intending to leave with me, or maybe someone was trying
to erase any sign that they were ever there. But there was
still the lingering possibility that I'd imagined it all.

In the confines of the cloakroom, I realized that I felt
safer than I had in hours. No one knew where I was. Maybe
they were looking for me, but for now I was alone. Nothing
made sense anymore, but at least in that dim, cramped space
nothing was getting worse. After I blew out the candle and

settled down there, I thought about everything Simon and Helena had told me. I was a superstitious person, but even a few days prior I'd have said that I didn't believe in ghosts. Now, no matter what Helena said, I knew. In this place, at least, they did exist.

From a huddled sitting position in the corner, I rolled onto my side with my head resting on my arm. Lying there, I watched the door and the ribbon of darkness at the bottom of it. Once I saw the light of dawn appear there, I thought, I'd get up, grab my things. and go look for Frances and Michael at Glass Bay. Until then, I could get the rest that had eluded me all night. At first, every tick and creak in the building made me twitch, but before long I calmed myself as I kept watching the gap under the door. If pale fingers slipped under it and started pulling it open, I would find a way to handle that.

For now, I was tired.

There were no dreams in those fitful hours, maybe because I never really slept. My mind wouldn't turn off, even as my body went limp and I felt powerless to move. I thought about what lay ahead, not just the following day but all the uncertain days beyond it. I was used to these late night spirals, but at other times at least I'd had my brother's company.

Even if I could get the children away from the lodge, I had no money left, and it would be a long journey home. When I thought back to the man who'd hired me, that silver-haired stranger with the resounding voice, I couldn't call his face to mind. I couldn't even picture his office. All I could

THE GUEST CHILDREN 237

conjure was a shadow in an empty space, giving me a good reason to leave the city. I wondered why Helena had asked me about that, but some part of me didn't want to know.

I'm not sure how long I slept, but I roused when I heard footsteps outside the door. There were whispers too, what sounded like a woman and a child. I felt foolish hiding, and I rose to my feet. In the gap under the door, I could see the glow of a lantern, steady and unflickering, as whoever held it approached the door. I was stupidly cornered, my heart beating as hard as it would when I heard the rattle of Mr. Sturgess's belt on the farm.

The footsteps stopped outside the cloakroom. There was a long silence, and then someone spoke my name. I knew Theresa's voice, but she sounded gentle now, almost maternal.

"Yes," I said.

"Are we playing hide-and-seek?"

"What have you done with the children's things?"

"We threw them out ages ago. Come out of there."

There was nothing else to be done. I opened the door, squinting in the light of the lantern as Theresa stood before me. I thought I saw movement behind her.

"Who's with you—?"

"Never mind," she said, raising the lantern to shine in my face. "In your room, what did Simon tell you?"

I shielded my eyes. "He told me that someone killed your son."

"It's not true."

"I don't know who to believe."

"Believe *me*. Come."

She motioned for me to follow, and I did, trailing the pool of light she cast as she crossed the ballroom and went out through the lobby into the dining room. The lights were out in there too. She sat at a table and set the lantern atop it. Sitting opposite her, I had a view out the window to the darkness and a wall of trees just outside the window.

"I wouldn't look out there. You might not like what you see."

"What is it you think I'm going to see?"

"Only you can know that, Randall." She reached for my hand, but I yanked it away from her. She looked wounded. I saw her eyes flit to someplace behind me, and she shook her head as if warning someone away.

Fighting the urge to look back there, I asked her a question instead. "Who killed Gerald?"

After a slow blink, she sighed. "It was an accident. A terrible accident, years ago. And you should leave it alone."

"Then that's what I'll do. I'm going to collect the children and take them away."

She laughed at me then. It felt like the first honest response she'd given me since I arrived the day before. I saw a figure then, at least one, move through the tree trunks in the forest outside the window. Theresa noticed my glance.

"I told you not to look out there."

"They can't hurt me."

THE GUEST CHILDREN 239

"They can. Believe me, they can." In the lantern's gleam, I could see tears in her eyes, but she didn't blink or wipe them away.

"I know Gerald is one of them."

Theresa slammed her hand on the table. "Stop saying his name." The look on her face then, the shining madness in her eyes . . . it was something beyond even the fury I'd seen in Simon when he attacked me in the dark.

"I'm going to leave now. With Frances and Michael, and with Helena. You can't do anything to stop us. None of you can."

Theresa sighed, just as the trees swayed outside the window. It was as if the forest sighed with her. She motioned to the screened porch. "Well. On your way, then."

"Thank you for your hospitality. I'll be sure to share my experiences here with the Hawksby family, their lawyer, and the police."

"As you wish."

Leaving her, I went upstairs again. I thought I heard her tearfully whispering to someone as I ventured into my room and closed the door. There was a fine layer of sand over everything now. Standing still a moment, I listened. I didn't hear Theresa coming after me or anyone else moving in the house, though I doubted that any of its residents was asleep. All I could hear were the small, dark waves rippling against the shore of Blank Lake. I'd be happy to be rid of the lake and its strange, fetid odour. Happier still to be rid of the lodge and its inhabitants.

Shaking out my things, I packed up my case again and fixed the rope straps over my shoulders. Instantly, I could feel the scabs start to tear from the friction. Through the curtains, I could tell it was not yet light, but it had to be soon. I couldn't wait any longer.

As I left the room, the door stuck again as it had the first time I tried to leave. The sense of panic that surged in me then was so powerful, my vision went into a blur and my breath stopped, but I dug my heels in and pulled it free, nearly tumbling back from the effort.

Out in the hall, I looked up and down, but there was no one about. Walking softly down to Helena's room, I tapped on the door. There was nothing for a few moments and I almost left, until I heard her whispered response.

"It's Randall. I'm leaving. I'm going to find the children. Come and meet us at Glass Bay."

There was silence for a moment. It was risky being out in the hall where anyone could come out to block my exit, and I kept eyeing the line of closed doors on either side.

Then Helena said, "Oh."

"Will you come?"

"I don't think so."

"But . . . you said you wanted to leave."

"I hope you get away," she said. "I do."

I heard her soft footsteps and then the creak of bed-springs as she lay down. There was nothing more to be done. I couldn't wait for her. Lingering for one last moment,

THE GUEST CHILDREN   241

I hoped she would come back and open the door or say something. She didn't.

Theresa was gone when I came back down the lobby stairs and crossed through the screened-in porch. I looked around for her, not to say goodbye but because I wanted to know where she was, for my own good. After her reaction to me talking about Gerald, the lunacy I'd seen in her eyes in that moment, I couldn't be sure her willingness to let me leave was sincere. For all I knew, she was hiding in wait with a kitchen knife.

Through the darkened garden I went, the paving stones slick now with a light, steady rain that felt greasy under my feet. The sound of it falling on the rocks and on the trees clustered around the lodge seemed to grow louder the further I went, as if it was hissing in protest of my departure. Passing the boathouse, I peered inside to ensure Michael and Frances weren't hiding in there. They weren't, but there was someone in the shadows, a tall male figure. I couldn't see his face, and he didn't move when my eyes found him. He stayed where he was, still as stone, but I could feel that he knew I was there. The only thing to do was get away. I didn't want anything to do with this. Fleeing the boathouse, I spotted someone on the dock waving to me.

Even in the dark, I could tell it was Julian. He waved to me, urgently, as if he had something important to tell me. I approached him with caution, wondering what he was doing in the pre-dawn black, wondering why he was always there, staring out across the water.

242 Patrick Tarr

Maybe he was trying to help me escape. He didn't seem to want me around, after all. As I went to him, my footfalls on the dock seemed to reverberate off the sheets of Shield rock around the lake and reflect back at me, loud as cracks of thunder.

Julian waited until I arrived. When I reached him, I felt his eyes searching mine.

"Bad night," he said. It was not a question.

"I'm going. I'm taking the children."

"Then I suppose this is goodbye. But I wanted you to see them."

"See who?"

Julian reached down to the dock and scratched a match across the surface, leaving a black scar across the planks. He lit a lantern and held it out from the end of the dock, shining it in a slow-moving arc over the dark water.

"Them," he said.

I didn't want to look, but I did.

Standing across the surface of the lake, some close and some many yards away, was a collection of men in military uniforms. Many were not even men, just boys. Some wore gas masks. A number of them had their hands raised in surrender. Blood pattered softly into the water from their many wounds. I felt their eyes all turn to me as one. Their looks felt like stones thrown into a mirror. I stumbled back, my feet nearly carrying me off the edge of the dock.

"Who are they?"

"I killed them," Julian said. "Didn't want to, with some

THE GUEST CHILDREN

of them. Sometimes didn't mean to. But I did. They come to be with me here. More of them all the time."

Their eyes on me, so black and so hollow, made me want to run away—but I was rooted in place, and I could no longer believe that running would get me anywhere.

"What do they want?"

"It's not about them. It's about me. Haven't you seen that yet?"

Julian turned towards me. I didn't like the look on his face, and took a step away from him, my ankle turning on the edge of the dock.

"You know what I'm talking about."

Maybe I did know. That figure I saw standing high in the trees earlier that day, the one I'd seen waving to me from the surface of the lake and just now in the boathouse, maybe that was what Julian was talking about. Even as I thought about it, I sensed that presence behind me at that moment on the dock. I wanted to turn and look, but I was afraid of what I'd see.

"I'm going now."

Before I could make a move, Julian shook his head, then surged forward and swung the lantern at my face. It happened so fast that I couldn't dodge it in time. The lamp struck me, oil exploding over my face as I fell backwards. I didn't even have a chance to take a breath before the dark water pulled me in.

★　★　★

CHAPTER 30

When I opened my eyes, I was on that same beach of all my nightmares, once again. The sand was pock-marked with craters and criss-crossed with barbed wire, but there were no bodies now, only me. As always, smoke crawled over everything, a predatory slowness to its advance. I rose to my hands and knees from the water and crawled up to the sand. There was a part of me that wanted to call out for help, but I didn't know who I'd be calling to, and I was afraid of who might answer. I just stood there in the water, under an oppressive sky and silence.

Since I didn't know what else to do, I started to walk. The dust and the smoke slithered across the beach and over-took me. I couldn't see much beyond my own searching hands in front of my face. Blind as I was, I staggered into a crater, tumbling down into red water. As always in my dreams, I tried to climb my way out, but the sand kept giv-ing way under my hands. The more I tried to pull myself up, the closer I came to burying myself alive. I kept

THE GUEST CHILDREN 245

scrambling anyway, the sand falling into my face and blinding me. Soon I was winded from exertion, and the sick blood-and-fuel smell was so overpowering that I could barely breathe. When I peered up again, the lip of the hole was further away than ever.

And there was a shadow looking down on me.

It was a soldier. He reached down a bloodied hand to help me climb out. I took it, feeling my body lifted back to the surface like a sack of flour. Once I was out, I collapsed on the beach, coughing. It took an eternity until my lungs found a cadence again, like old boyhood nightmares when I couldn't remember how to run, the rhythm constantly escaping me just as I found it.

When the panic subsided, I was looking at a pair of combat boots planted in the sand next to my face. Struggling to my feet, I looked at the man standing before me. Under his dented helmet was a shifting mass of sand where his face was meant to be. It swirled and rippled as if trying to form into human features. His uniform was torn, as was the flesh underneath it.

Even without a face, I was sure it wasn't Emil. In the heart of me, I knew who it was. He walked away across the landscape, and I followed. There was no choice in it anymore. Everything that had happened since I left the apartment for the train station that day was leading to this moment. I trailed the soldier's footsteps through the beach, stepping over bodies and barbed wire and chunks of burning wood. Sometimes I almost lost him in the smoke.

When I looked back from the beach across the black water, I thought I saw Glass Bay on the other side, the narrow strip of beach and the Sand Palace there, and that long flight of stairs. It seemed like we walked for hours, until finally we came to a mound in the sand. The soldier stopped there. Falling to my knees, I knew what I was meant to do.

I started to dig, the sand like fine-sharded glass, biting into my skin. I dug until I felt fabric and flesh, and then gently uncovered the body waiting there. When I got to the face, it was partly gone. Shrapnel had peeled pieces of it away to the bone. The poor dead soldier's mouth and eyes were open and filled with sand.

I looked up at the man standing next to me.

He seemed a hundred feet tall, looming over me with an endless charcoal sky at his back. There was no reaction, no shift in his features, yet somehow I knew there was more he expected from me. I dragged the body out of its tomb of sand and onto the beach. Arranging the corpse carefully, I straightened his legs out and folded his arms over his chest.

I saw the dog tags then. I didn't want to look, but my hands moved against my will. Reaching inside the dead man's tunic, I tugged on the chain and read the name embossed on the tags.

EDWARD JOHN STURGESS.

A choked laugh came out of me, rippled across the silent landscape.

The Guest Children   247

My brother was a shut-in, an addled mess of damage, delusion, and drink. No army in the world would put him in a uniform. It was impossible that he'd join up, more impossible still that he'd make it through training and find his way to the front. But I knew there was something here, that this wasn't a trick. The longer I sat with the body, the more I believed it to be true. All that I'd seen since I arrived at Glass Bay pointed to this, a thing I'd tried so hard to deny. My brother died, alone and choking on sand, in some distant battle on some distant beach.

Edward was gone. I'd mourned him. I'd missed him. I'd convinced myself that the events that led Edward to this place were not my fault. Sitting there, I closed my eyes and I sent myself flying back to the city, back to the darkness of our shared room. Edward was there, waiting for me by the window. When he saw me there, he said something I'd heard him say once before.

"You left me, Rand."

And with those words, I remembered everything.

★ ★ ★

Chapter 31

My brother and I were snatched as young boys from a life on the streets of London. Our father died in the Great War. Whatever became of our mother, we could never be certain. We only knew what we were told, which may have been a lie. We were carried away to Canada and sent to live on the Sturgess farm, where it was expected that we'd have a proper Christian upbringing, and that we'd work to earn it. We lived in a remote community, where we were strange and wild and not at all like the other boys. It was a hard life, but my brother and I looked after each other.

Until that one time out in the woods when he needed me, and I ran away. I should have stayed by Edward's side. After that, he was never the same.

All these things were true.

After we fled the Sturgess house, we walked and hitched and rode the rails before landing in the city. It wasn't a good time to be looking for work. It wasn't a good time

THE GUEST CHILDREN 249

for anything. By then, Edward was already a burden. There was something about his countenance, and the way he spoke, that led people to an instant and violent dislike. Edward gave it right back to them. He turned to drink again and pursued it with abandon. He was prone to violent outbursts when he felt cornered, and he felt cornered most of the time.

I was more capable, able to muster some manners when needed, and I was a hard worker. I think I might have done great things with my life, if not for the fact that I was saddled with Edward. But because of that moment I left him behind in the woods, I never complained. My lapse made Edward into what he'd become, so I had to protect him.

We struggled in the city, sleeping in a shack in the valley for a time, living off scrounged, begged, and stolen food. When the war began, things started to change for us.

I took on whatever work I could get, but by then the pressure to enlist was growing. Many of the jobs for able-bodied young men were given to the women lining up to help with the war effort, the rest were subject to regulations. For me to enlist would be the end of Edward's security, so it was never a choice. I managed to keep money coming in, took the accusations of cowardice from everyone around me on the chin, and I promised I'd never leave him alone.

When I met Mildred, Edward was threatened. I spent more time away from him, and he spent more time inside, alone. The longer he spent in our room, the less willing he was to leave. I never left him without food or books, but without me there, something in him started to spoil.

When I told Edward that I'd asked Mildred to marry me, he slid into a new and bottomless darkness. Sulking and seething, he made our tiny room feel even smaller, so much space taken up with his foul temper. He was certain I'd abandon him, hurt that I'd do so after a lifetime together in our war against the world. I'd never have done that. I just needed to figure out a way that I could keep taking care of him while living another life, the one I wanted for myself.

Edward was so wounded by my betrayal that he got drunk and went to enlist. It was February 1944. Somehow, he must have got through all their tests and questions. They were desperate for new men by then, in the lead-up to D-Day and the end of it all.

I couldn't picture my brother keeping his anger and dark thoughts tamped down in an interview with stolid military men, his speaking tone even and his thoughts collected. But he must have pulled it off, because he left there with enlistment papers in hand.

Edward was waiting for me in the apartment when I got home, and I could tell he'd been drinking. He shoved the papers in my face and told me I wouldn't have to take care of him anymore. I could have my lousy life with Mildred, a fleapit house, and scores of dirty, stupid children. I could forget he ever existed. But he, at least, would be a hero. The thought of my brother in the war made my legs shake

THE GUEST CHILDREN   251

and sent cold steel shavings through my belly. My panic pushed me to tears. We didn't speak all through that night. When I woke the next morning, Edward was gone.

I never saw him again.

For a while I tried to write letters telling the military of their mistake. I went to the recruitment centre and made such a scene, I nearly ended up in jail. I did my best to find out where Edward would be training so I could warn his commanding officer that my brother wasn't fit to serve. None of it worked. No one would help.

So, I waited for news.

After the first telegram came from the Casualty Officer, telling me of Edward John Sturgess's death, I stopped going outside. More came after that, letters of condolence from military and government officials, even a card from the King and Queen.

Through all it, I forgot about Mildred. She called on the shared line, leaving messages with the neighbours, then came over a few times and pounded on the door. I couldn't bear for her to see me in the state I was in. I told her through the door that I didn't have time for her. I had to look after my brother, who'd become unwell. There was no space left in my life for her.

"I don't want to see you anymore," I told her.

I never even told her that Edward was dead, because speaking it aloud would have made it real. It didn't take long for her to give up, and only a few months later I learned she'd married someone else. I stayed inside, papered over the windows. Apart from weekly trips to the corner grocer in the early morning, I saw no one.

Almost no one.

Because the thing was, my bond with Edward, the blood pact of our shared history, those things wouldn't die so easily. Nothing about my brother was ever easy. He returned late one night in October 1944. I woke up in my cot, the air frigid in the apartment, and saw Edward Sturgess lying on the other bed and watching me, the way he used to do after I came home from work.

"Can't sleep?" he said.

There was a choice before me then—a choice to deny the spectre I saw before me, or simply to accept him and go back to a time when the weight of guilt didn't perch on my chest in my waking hours and pursue me through my nightmares.

I chose acceptance.

I got up to fix a drink. We talked into the night about what we were going to do. We were out of money, living on soda crackers, and something needed to change. I needed to look after my brother, as I'd been doing for most of my life. It was very important that I not go to war. After all, I couldn't look after Edward anymore if something happened to me.

"If we have to leave here, I think I'll die," he told me.

That was the thing that finally got me out of the apartment.

"I'll find something soon, all right?"

Edward stayed back, as Edward always did in our later

days, and I went out looking for work. I'd barely been outside in weeks. My eyes screamed in the daylight, and the nearness of other people made me twitch. But I knew I couldn't fail.

Even though everyone said the war was winding down by then, I had to find myself a job that could keep me secure on the home front. Those jobs still weren't too easy to come by. I asked around and then asked around some more, until finally I got someone to introduce me to Clarence. I had to give him a cut of my wages to secure my place on the crew, but I got the job, and I got to keep Edward alive, passing the time between shifts with him in the shadows of our room. It was always easier to believe the lie in the dark. That's why I papered over the windows.

When I got back after my first day building houses, Edward was waiting. He was proud of me for getting the job, relieved that we wouldn't find ourselves out on the street. I was relieved too. I wanted to embrace him then, but I was afraid what would happen if I did.

Before long, our life together became such a drab and exhausting routine that I no longer remembered the truth. A lie would feel remarkable, and my long days on the job site and restless nights in the flat with my brother were anything but remarkable. I didn't question why Edward would never leave the room, or why no one else was allowed to see him. In a deeper place, I knew that as long as I played by those rules, I still had a family.

And that was all I'd ever wanted.

CHAPTER 32

I woke up, gasping in the dark. My face was wet with lake water or tears, I couldn't be sure which. My throat felt raw and ragged as if I'd been screaming in my sleep, just as Julian had told me I was prone to do. Trying to move, I realized I was lying face down on wooden planks. From the sound and the smell of my surroundings, I was in the boathouse. But I wasn't sure if I was alone, or if someone watched me from somewhere in the shadows.

Sitting up, still dripping wet in my clothes, I tried to tell myself that everything I'd remembered about Edward was a dream. But I knew that it wasn't. I knew it through my soaked and shivering skin all the way to the dank, chilled hollows of my bones. Helena told me that this place could show you your lost ones. I could see now that it didn't matter if you'd convinced yourself that they weren't lost, it would show you all the same.

My brother was dead. He wasn't waiting for me in our apartment, mumbling about imminent invasions and

THE GUEST CHILDREN   255

drinking spiked coffee. He wasn't going to berate me when
I came home for taking too long away, nor was he going to
keep me awake pacing the room all night. He was gone,
and I'd driven Mildred away. I had no one and nothing to
claim in life.

But I did have something to do.

As I rose to my feet, legs shaking, I felt a sting in the
raw skin on my face where the lamp oil burned before I fell
in the water. Remembering Julian's attack, I raised my
hands to my shoulders in case another ambush should
come at me from the dark. Scanning the shadows, I knew
I wasn't alone, even before I spotted the figure standing a
few feet away from me. There was a feeling, like a cold
finger stroking the back of my neck.

The person who came forward into a shaft of light was
not who I expected, and the sight of him turned my shivering into a full jelly-legged dread. A small sound escaped
me, a shamefully boyish and frightened sound. I started
backing away as he came to me.

"Randall," Mr. Sturgess said.

I couldn't tell if he said it out loud or if the sound of my
name was only in my head. Mr. Sturgess stepped closer
still, and I could see that damage to his face, the caved-in
cheekbone where Edward hit him with the log, the ruin of
his right eye socket.

"No," I said.

Mr. Sturgess smiled then, and silently slipped the brown
leather belt out of the loops in his trousers. "I told her you'd

be useless. Gutter boys, who'd never work hard. Never speak without uttering falsehoods. And I was right, wasn't I."

He was closer now, the sour smell of the lake so over-powering I thought I might black out. Mr. Sturgess was near enough to lash out with that belt, but I was backed up to the wall.

"You couldn't even take care of your own brother. Too yellow to fight for your country like I did. Useless."

The voice sounded so much like my memory of him. The kind of things he'd tell us when the belt came out. The sting and the shame when he made me believe what he said. The thing about Edward was, he never did believe them. Mr. Sturgess never got to him like he got to me.

Helena, the children, they'd told me these spectres weren't real. In that moment, I didn't believe it. Sturgess was as real as I remembered him, the real man we left for dead in a snowy farmyard, never to return. Seeing him likely meant he was dead by now, but then again, maybe it didn't mean that at all. Maybe it only meant he was still alive in my worst memories.

When he raised the belt, I ducked around him and ran. Shoes thudding across the deck planks, I went out the door. As I emerged, Simon and Julian were coming my way. They tried to grasp at me, but I pushed Simon into the water and knocked Julian down. He cried out as I grabbed my suitcase, sitting sodden outside the boathouse. Simon screamed my name in a rage from the water. In a moment, I was running again.

THE GUEST CHILDREN   257

When I reached the trailhead, I paused for a moment, as frightened of what lay ahead of me as I was of what I'd just escaped. It was darker than the rest of the night in the forest, a place that had tormented me even in daylight.

But I only stopped for a moment. I could hear Simon and Julian calling out my name back by the lodge, and soon Theresa's voice joined the chorus. The suitcase over my shoulders again, I sprinted through the woods, hurtling over tree roots and protruding stone. Branches whipped at my stinging face and I turned my ankle on uneven terrain more than once, tumbling to the ground. Each time, as I rose, I sensed figures gathering in the shadows around me and heard their murmurings, like stirrings of dead leaves. Unable to bear any more horrors that night, I ran until I blacked out.

When I came to, I was standing on the beach at Glass Bay. I'd made it along the trail and down the steps somehow. Placing my sodden suitcase down, I looked up at the steps and around the beach. I was alone there on the sand, wet and shivering in the cool rain. Rather, I thought I was alone at first—but when I moved towards the Sand Palace to look inside, two shadows detached from behind humps of stone and came towards me.

Michael and Frances. Their presence should have been a relief, but the way their eyes shone in the darkness made me take a step away from them.

"We knew you'd come," Frances said.

"I wasn't sure you'd be here."

Michael came up closer and peered at me. I could see now just how skinny and malnourished he was. His hair was a greasy tangle, and there was a battlefield of bug bites across his face and bare arms. When Frances approached as well, I could see she didn't look much better. Her hair was knotted and her face so thin it was almost skeletal. It was like when Edward and I were living rough, the worst of it when our ribs would show through our too-small shirts.

"It's almost light," I said. "We should go."

"Not yet," Frances said.

"Simon and the others, I think they've followed me. We don't have much time."

"We need to finish saying goodbye."

"No, please don't."

But the children ignored me, moving past me along the beach. Their feet shuffled through the sand as they passed and I saw that they were barefoot. Even in the dark I could see how dirty and scarred those feet were. I tried to grasp Michael's shoulder, but he pulled away from me. Though he was thin, he was wiry, and I no longer had the strength to fight.

They moved towards the Sand Palace. The fact that I'd finally gotten away from the lodge only to be confronted with this small, haunted replica of it filled me with the panic of a trapped animal. I heard the drainpipe sound again, coming from inside the playhouse, as the Hawksbys climbed the short ladder to the platform. Michael went second, and when

THE GUEST CHILDREN 259

he got to the top, he looked back and waved for me to follow. I didn't want to go inside, but I went to look.

I wished I hadn't. With my eyeline right around the same level as the platform, I saw the children scuttle across the uneven planks to sit in the corner.

They weren't alone.

Two other figures sat across from them. I could see that it was a man and a woman, the tarnished-penny gleam of their eyes as they both silently turned to peer at me. The man had a leg bent out at an unnatural angle, but I could see that he was smiling. The woman's dark hair hung down over her face. She eyed me through it like a beaded curtain.

Their parents, of course. The late Mr. and Mrs. Hawksby. I did not want to bear witness, but I couldn't allow the children to take too long about whatever this business would be. Michael started to cry, and Frances patted him with a dirty hand. Their parents, or these twisted shadows of them, observed but said nothing.

"We must say goodbye, Michael," Frances said. "You know it's time."

"We won't see them anymore."

"That's right. We have to go back to London. It's where we belong, not here."

Looking at me, Michael leaned close to his sister and whispered something in her ear. It was a habit Edward used to have with me when we needed to discuss important matters in front of strangers. They were like us in so many ways.

Frances listened and nodded, then looked at me. "Michael wants you to step away, Mr. Sturgess. He doesn't want you to hear what he's going to say."

I was glad to be away from the sight of them. The two things inside the Sand Palace turned as one to watch me move away. I shuddered from the feel of their gaze as I sat down in the sand near the base of the playhouse and waited.

For a few minutes, I heard the children whispering. Even with the rain falling and soaking me through, I wanted to lie down and go to sleep. It would be so easy. I could be shut of the terrors of the day, even for a little while. But I knew that if I did that, I'd never leave.

There was crying then, and I heard someone kicking or thumping inside the playhouse. The whole structure shuddered. Finally, Frances came out of there. She was practically dragging Michael behind her, and he fell off the ladder to the ground.

Once he was out, the spell seemed to be broken. Michael took one last look inside, then turned his gaze to me sitting on the beach at the base of the playhouse and cocked his head.

"Are you talking to the Wet Boy?"

"What?"

"Gerald, he lives under the house. That's where he's buried."

THE GUEST CHILDREN

261

"How do you know?"

Frances answered me. "We had an idea about where he might be. He gave us some hints. Like a game. So we dug, and we found him. When Theresa found out, that's when we had to run away for good. She was so angry that we'd stirred him up."

I looked down into the narrow gap under the structure, imagining the bones of the poor child down there. Simon had built this monument to his dead son right on top of the boy's corpse.

"Do you know how he died?"

"It's terrible," Michael said.

Frances sighed, as if telling me about it was a chore. "Gerald dug himself a big pit in the beach. He wanted to have a playhouse, but his father wouldn't build him one. So he made a pit instead. And he dug it very deep."

"Right here in this exact place," Michael said.

"He spent all day on it, and part of the next, with tools from the lodge. When his father found him there, the pit was so deep there was water coming in at the bottom and he was getting cold. That's why, when you see him, he has blue lips."

"No, that's because he's *dead*," Michael said.

Frances waved him off. "Uncle Simon was so cross with Gerald, because he'd ruined his best suit of clothes with all the sand and the water. So, Uncle Simon left him there to punish him, and told him to get out on his own."

"But he couldn't."

"No, he couldn't. When he tried to climb out, the walls of the pit collapsed on him, and he ended up buried alive."

"Drowned in sand," I said.

"Too awful," Michael said. "They just said some words and filled in the rest of the hole. And now Gerald leaves sand wherever he goes."

Frances beckoned me to lean closer to her. When I did, she whispered into my ear. Her words came in cool puffs of breath. "Sometimes I wonder if the people and things we've seen here are all really just Gerald. Even our parents. He doesn't want to be alone, so he shows people things to make them stay. He's very lonely here, he told me. But I couldn't tell Michael that, because he wouldn't believe me."

Michael frowned at her from a few feet away. "We said no secrets."

I thought about the sand crater and the soldier of my dreams. So many pieces of my many nightmares seemed to have led me to this place, but I didn't have time to think about what was behind it. Rising, feeling the exhaustion of the long night in my bones, I stood over the children.

"It's time to go."

CHAPTER 33

I left my suitcase behind. Still, after the long night, the trip up the rain-slick stairs was almost more than I could handle. I hadn't slept properly in days, and between the visions and my nightmares, I could no longer tell the difference between sleep and waking. As we went up the steps, the children leading the way and all of us spaced out evenly, I kept thinking that we wouldn't be allowed to go. What would stop us, I couldn't be sure, but I felt it coming. Breathless from the climb, I expected the whole staircase to dislodge from the rock face and topple us back into Glass Bay. At least that would be an end to it all.

I looked at my watch, hoping dawn would come soon, but it had finally stopped from my time in the water. It might have been thirty minutes or three hours since I was pushed from the dock. Once we got back to the top, me panting, sweating, and near sick from the climb, I looked back down at the dark void of the bay, expecting to see someone watching us from below. But all I saw was the bay, narrow and pointed, like the outline of a blade stabbed into the rocky shoreline. The Sand Palace, that haphazard, bedevilled replica of Glass Point Lodge, showed no pale faces peering out of its window. I hoped this would be the last time I ever saw it.

As we went, there was a part of me that wondered why I hadn't seen him yet. All the other spectres about, yet no sign of my brother. I didn't know if that was out of spite or mercy, but in either case I was glad I hadn't had to face him. There was no way I could bear it.

We had to first walk back towards the lodge to reach the trail I thought would take us away from there. I felt a quickening in the air, as if the forest itself knew of our plan to escape and was determined to prevent it. I felt it in the rustling of the leaves, in the sudden silence of the birds and insects, and in a drop of temperature that raised the hair on my arms. As we walked, I started to see moving shadows along the trail.

"Do you see them too?" I asked.

"Don't look," Michael said.

"I'm not afraid."

"Are you sure?"

"Yes."

"Then why didn't you go to war?"

"Michael, please shut up," Frances hissed at her brother, but he merely shrugged off her rebuke and kept walking.

"I had my reasons," I said.

"That's what our father said."

"No, Michael, he said he was too old and that he was doing important things for the country in his own way. And for us."

"Same thing," Michael said.

I was aware by then that something in the woods was following us. I could hear movement in our wake, see sliding shadows in the periphery of my vision. Instead of slowing, or turning to face it, I tried to think of something to drive me forward.

I thought about Mildred.

It wouldn't be easy, but if I told her the truth of what happened with Edward, and if she hadn't yet found someone else, maybe I could convince her to take me back. I thought about that day on the streetcar, the way she looked at me with that soul-piercing mix of pity and derision. How, after I climbed off the car, she stood watching me from the window with her friends.

One foot in front of the other, I tried to imagine that I could make it happen. But to tell Mildred the truth would be to confess to an instability of mind that I knew she could never abide. She was wonderfully, proudly normal. And if I was being honest with myself, the only reason she'd had any interest in me in the first place was that I'd hidden so much of myself and my past from her. I'd never even let her meet my brother.

"Who is that?" I heard Frances say. "There's a woman in the trees."

I answered without looking. "Someone I know."

"Did she die?"

"I don't think so."

"But you lost her."

"Yes."

"She's not really here," Frances said. "But you want her to be."

Michael said, "It's why people can't leave."

Something shifted inside me, some unseen force pushing my organs up into my chest, bound for my throat. Grabbing the children's hands more roughly than I meant to, I dragged them along the path behind me. Michael whined complaints, but I ignored them.

At one point, my foot caught in a fissure in the rock, and I stumbled. Before I fell, the children steadied me. I bit my lip to ground myself in pain, something real, and we carried along the Glass Bay trail to where it merged with the one that led from the lodge.

When we reached the junction, I heard someone coming our way. Picking up a damp length of broken branch from the forest floor, I held it like a club and waited to see who it was. Probably Simon and Julian, with whom I still had unfinished business.

The children looked up as I pushed them behind me. There was no fear in their eyes. I imagined they had none left to spare after all the time they'd spent in this place. The footsteps grew nearer, coming around a bend into view. My grip tightened on the branch. I wondered if I was going to die, and if it would matter to anyone if I did.

The Guest Children 267

It was Helena. She came into view, walking at a determined pace and carrying her suitcase. Emil followed behind her, matching her every step with one of his own.

She kept turning around, telling him to stop, telling him not to follow. Emil would obey, but the moment she turned around again, he'd start after her once more. Helena cried, shouted, and begged for him to stop, but he didn't stop. As I waited there for her, I felt I was watching something too forbidden, too private to be shared. But I wasn't about to leave her behind.

Helena let out an anguished scream that resounded through the forest. I was sure she'd be heard all the way over at the marina. With the cry still tearing out of her, Helena pushed her husband away. Emil staggered back, teetering on his heels with those gas mask eyes staring at his wife, and then he fell.

When he hit the ground, Emil's body snapped into a pile of dark sand that collapsed and spread across the forest floor like a bloodstain. Helena sank to her knees, running her hands through the mound of it and whispering in German.

I told the children to follow behind me as I approached her. Helena didn't hear us coming, so when I reached out for her, whispering her name, she shouted and swung an open hand in my direction. I dodged it and grabbed her to keep her from falling over. Helena blinked when she saw me, and her eyes went wide when she saw the children.

"We're going now," I said. "Out through the woods. We're going."

"I was looking for you."

"Leave your belongings behind. We need to move quickly."

"Do you think we can get away?"

I couldn't answer that with certainty, so I said, "I hope we can."

Helena nodded and I could see her trying not to look at the pile of sand. I didn't think we'd seen the last of Emil, nor of any of the others. Not if we lingered here for too long. She leaned down to look at the children, touching them to make sure they were real. Frances seemed to take to her immediately, but Michael ducked away.

"I've seen you before," Michael told her. "You were the last to come."

"I thought I'd seen you too, but . . ."

"You thought we were dead."

"Yes."

Frances and Michael both nodded. I heard movement in the woods and saw something duck behind a tree trunk about a hundred yards away.

"Where have you been all this time?" Helena asked.

"Nowhere," Frances told her.

"Then let's get you somewhere now," Helena said.

We set out in the direction of the road, hoping the sun would come up soon. It felt as if the forest still had a stranglehold over the dawn, throttling it back to keep us in its thrall. My yearning for light wasn't rooted in any certainty that it would make us safe—I knew that it wouldn't—but only because it would be easier to stay on the path and find our way out.

I led the way, followed by Frances and Michael, with Helena in the rear. I could hear Helena softly crying between our footfalls, and I remembered her sorrow when she pushed Emil down and he ceased to be. I thought of Helena, because I didn't want to think about Mildred again, or Edward, or Mr. Sturgess. There was something rising in me I didn't want to face, a jarring and discordant feeling that had been inside me ever since I'd arrived at this place.

Once more, I saw something stalking us through the rain-shrouded trees. I still carried the branch by my side to defend us, but I didn't know what good a piece of wood would do against things that were already dead.

Ahead, I saw the path dipping down into a wetland, a decaying wooden swamp bridge leading through a depression in the landscape where the ground was submerged under fetid standing water. The light rain falling into the swamp made a sizzling sound. I stopped to look at the bridge, hoping it would hold us all, and wondered why I had no memory of crossing it on my approach to the lodge.

I couldn't see the end of the bridge as it wound its way through the woods, and I didn't know where it would lead. The tree canopy swayed above us, those pallid leaves shuddering in a way that sounded like mocking laughter.

"Is something wrong?" Helena asked from behind me.

"I don't remember this bridge from when I came in. I don't know if it's safe to pass."

"It's the only way out, isn't it?"

"I think it must be."

"I'm not turning back."

That was enough for me. I got moving again, following the sloping trail down until my feet hit the sodden wood of the bridge. After we walked along the boards for a few minutes, I saw something moving in the rippling water alongside me. I hurried my pace, but I saw the swamp's displacement match my speed, the flash of a pale face under the surface.

"Don't look," Michael said.

I did as I was told, my feet thumping across the boards. I dreaded the cold, damp clutch of a hand coming up to grab my ankle through a breach. Soon, I was walking so fast that Helena called for me to slow down. I thought I saw a bit of a blue tinge above the tree canopy as we carried on. Maybe the dawn would come soon after all, and this night would finally end.

Just as I started moving again, I felt footsteps reverberating along the bridge. There was someone coming up behind us in the dark.

"Who is that?"

Helena looked down the bridge into the black behind us. "We don't want to know. We must keep moving."

Frances looked up at me, pleading. "Mrs. Heitmann is right."

I looked to Michael, but he just stared back at me. He knew very well, I think, what was following us. And he

THE GUEST CHILDREN 271

knew it was coming for me. The trees around us started to sway and bow as if in some heavy wind, but there wasn't even a ripple in the swamp water.

The footsteps following us were getting closer, growing heavier. I was frightened, more frightened than I'd been since I'd come to Blank Lake. I wanted to run, to leave the children behind. They were nothing to me, just a job I no longer needed. I could leave this place forever. After all, I had no right to interfere in these things.

As the steps came thump-thump-thumping towards us, I heard faint splashes in the water. More shadows ducked in and around the trees. Something thrummed all around me, as if the whole swamp had a circulatory system quickening along with my heart. We could never outrun it. That was something I knew the moment I heard the approach.

I decided then that I'd had enough of running. I'd fled from the Sturgess farm, from the war, and from the death of my own brother. It was time to stop.

When I made the choice to remain and let them go on without me, it didn't feel like bravery, only surrender. When you get down to the core of it, maybe that's all bravery is— an acceptance that whatever will happen will happen, and your own life doesn't much matter in the course of things.

"You three carry on," I said. "Run along now, all right?"

Helena looked at me for a time, five heartbeats by my count, and then she nodded.

"We'll wait for you at the road," Helena said.

"Don't, just keep going."

"You know who's coming?" Frances said.

"Yes."

"Do you know that it won't really be them?"

That dissonant, wind-chime sound was so loud in my head that I could barely answer her.

"Yes."

"Thank you, Mr. Sturgess," Frances said.

Frances threw her arms around my waist and squeezed. Michael only blinked. Helena took Frances's hand to carry on along the bridge. Michael tugged my arm and motioned me to lean down. When I did, he whispered into my ear.

"You'll turn into one of them too, you know."

"Go on," I said.

Michael ran to catch up with Frances and Helena. As the sound of their departure faded into the darkness, I heard the footsteps coming from the other direction stop dead. The movement in the water and in the trees around me stopped as well. Even the rain stopped. There followed a silence of such weight I felt it squeezing the breath from my chest.

It was broken when someone called my name.

"Rand?"

I walked back along the bridge to meet this shadow wearing my brother's face. The blue light of the coming dawn was starting to chase off the darkness, but I could still see no end to the swamp. After I walked for a few paces,

THE GUEST CHILDREN 273

my breath up high and shallow and my heart shuddering, I saw a figure waiting for me on the bridge.

Edward didn't speak, he didn't wave, he only watched my approach with a faint smile. It was a smile that I'd not seen from him for so long, I had to fight back a surge of happiness. When I got close to him, the expression melted away.

"You left me, Rand."

"That's not true."

"I followed you. The day after you left. I bought a train ticket, with some of the money you left behind for me."

"No, you didn't."

"I didn't like the train, but I closed my eyes and plugged my ears, and it was okay. After that, I got a ride on a milk truck to Creekmont, and then I found my way here. It was hard going, and I was frightened. But I needed you."

"You died, Edward. You died in the war."

"In Creekmont, I spoke to that girl in the general store, the one with the spectacles. She was pretty, wasn't she? I thought she was."

"Why are you here?"

"I told you not to come. But you wouldn't listen to me—"

"You're not Edward."

Edward strode forward to put his hands on my shoulders. They felt warm and real. I could smell coffee and liquor on his breath. He leaned in and embraced me. The stubble from his unshaven face scraped against my cheek.

"I missed you. I was scared."

"You're lying."

I don't know what I expected from him, but he looked hurt. "Won't you come back and keep me company? You're all I've got."

"I don't think I want to do that."

In the echo chamber of the swamp, all I could hear was our breath, rising and falling. The coming dawn cast long shadows through the silver maple, tamarack, and black ash. Edward dropped his hands from my shoulders and looked at me. Once more he had that sly half smile of Edward's from when times were good. The same wild chaos I'd always seen in his eyes.

"You have nowhere else to go," he said. "I'm all you've got too."

★　★　★

PART 5

HOME

CHAPTER 34

When I open my eyes, I'm sitting on the floor of the Sand Palace. My palms are flat beside me on the slanted floor, cold grains of sand pressing into my flesh. Edward sits across from me. It's night, and so dark now that all I can see are flashes of his eyes and teeth in a moonbeam coming through a gap in the burlap. I don't want to be here again, but knowing that there is no place else to go makes it easier to endure.

"Hi Rand," Edward says.

"Stop. I know you're not him."

"We can talk, can't we?"

Without Helena here, I can no longer tell which visions are part of this place and which have sprung from the disintegration of my sanity. My brother is dead, and yet he is seated in this crooked little playhouse with me, and he is remembering the good things that happened to us, as few as they were. I think he wants to keep me here. He knows that if I leave this place, he will cease to be. But for all the good memories he conjures for my benefit, I see the bad ones too.

The bearded man outside our shack with his jaw hanging down from Mr. Sturgess's hatchet. Sturgess himself, writhing on the ground and screaming for our blood. A railroad man's club coming down on me as we raced away from the tracks. Edward kicked senseless and spitting blood in the back of some barroom. Months on end trapped in our tiny room in the city. Mildred sliding a note under the door—*Why can't I meet him?*

Finally, I see Edward waiting in our apartment for me to come back from Blank Lake, a trip home I will never make, for a reunion that will never come to pass. All those long nights in that tiny room, I was talking to a brother as false as the one before me now, one I'd built from my own grief and guilt, stitched together with the loose, dark threads of our memories.

After I while, I close my eyes to him. His voice drones on, falling into the usual pattern of paranoia and delusion—a turning and tumbling monologue that I thought for so long was his mind unspooling, when in truth it turned out to be my own. I don't want to hear any more, but I'm not ready to leave either.

Sometimes I wonder if Frances was right, and it's really just Gerald sitting with me, the lonely boy wearing my brother's face to keep me here. I guess it doesn't much matter to me one way or the other. Edward moves closer,

THE GUEST CHILDREN

his face is still in shadow, but I can feel his presence. He smells of wet sand.

"Please don't leave me alone, Rand," he says.

I reach out to take his hand. It's cold, but it's better than nothing.

*   *   *

CHAPTER 35

Within a couple of days, I settle into my new life at the lodge. I've found ways to do my part, helping tend to the garden and fixing little things around the building. I use a fine net to scoop up the little fish to eat, though I still have not acquired a taste for them. Sometimes I can snare a rabbit or a squirrel, a trick I remember from boyhood.

I don't have much to say to the others, nor they to me. The lodge is quiet through the days and nights we spend together. I see Agatha walking in the woods with the woman who follows her, the one Michael called the Red Lady. Sometimes they seem to speak, but much of the time they pass in silence. I see Julian out on the dock, focused on the spot on the water where his dead stand watching, and trying not to see anything else. We never speak of the night he attacked me with the lantern. We never speak at all. Even when the boat returns with some supplies, Julian stays where he is. No one wants to be here anymore, but no

THE GUEST CHILDREN 281

one will leave. All the strange ways of the guests seem normal to me now. We are all permanent residents of Glass Point, along with our companions. I merely had to let this place in, and now I am one of them.

When I'm not doing my part around the lodge or taking silent meals with the others, I sit by Blank Lake with Edward. Sometimes I tell stories of our younger days, but most often we simply sit there and watch the ever-changing weather. He asks little of me. It's easier than when he was alive, or when I still believed him to be. Apart from the twice-monthly boat visit, no one ever comes here. The days take on a numbing sameness that suits me fine.

I think about Mildred once in a while, and often I wonder what's become of Helena and the children. I hope they've returned home, and shed all memories of this place. Sometimes I hope someone will come to free me from Glass Point, as I did for them. But eventually, all thoughts of the outside world and the people in it fade away. For all I know, another war has begun by now. It makes no difference to us here.

One gloomy winter day, when I go out to check my snares, I find Simon hanging from a low tree branch by his belt. He's been there for some time, though Theresa has said nothing of his absence. I'm not sure any of us noticed he was gone. Theresa will not weep for her husband, as I know she still does for her child. And I know that I will see him again, lingering around the woods, haunting his wife and likely the rest of us too.

I cut Simon down with an old wood saw and then go back to the house to get help moving him. He's not far from Glass Bay, so I suggest we take him there to be with Gerald. The stairs are too precarious to carry him down, so we come to a silent agreement. Rolling him over the cliff with Julian, Agatha, and Theresa helping, we all flinch at the sound of his body hitting the beach. It's dark by the time we drag him up into the Sand Palace.

I light it on fire.

We don't say a prayer for him. We all just watch it burn, but I don't think any of us believe that destroying it will change anything. It's just a slapdash collection of wood and nails. It wasn't what kept our ghosts here, nor was it the lake or the lodge or even poor Gerald. It was only us. When we go, perhaps it will end. There is no one left alive who loves us. No one whose thoughts and longings will bring us back. No one to remember us at our passing. No one will even notice we're gone.

Edward watches me from the clifftop, and I'm happy to have him there. I'd always thought I was all he had left in the world, but in truth I had it backwards. When I leave here, he'll be gone forever. And I don't want that day to come just yet.

★ ★ ★

CHAPTER 36

When they came out of the woods onto the dusty sideroad, Helena started heaving for breath, tears spilling down her face. Frances was cross with her, as she was meant to be their guardian, but she went to console her anyway. Reminding Helena that she was their only hope of finding help, Frances asked her to pull herself together as kindly as she could manage.

Michael stood at the side of the road and stared into the trees, as if waiting for Randall or someone else to come out after him. He'd been quiet all through the endless walk out of the wilderness. Frances had to wonder if her brother hadn't turned himself off in some way, closed a door that had been open in his mind for far too long. More than likely, he was thinking about their mum and dad, and she could hardly blame him for that.

When Helena rose from her knees and wiped her face, she forced a smile and said, "Time to walk. Please follow me, perhaps we'll find some food."

Michael did perk up at the mention of food. Helena led the way. They walked despite the blisters, the heat, and the bugs that came out of the trees to bite at their necks and faces. They walked through thirst. Helena found some edible weeds by the side of the road, but they did little to stave off the trembling Frances felt in her legs.

When they heard the engine behind them, Helena pushed them to the side of the road and then stood in the middle of it until a delivery truck came to a halt. She lied to the driver about who they were. Frances thought the man knew that Helena was lying, because he put her in the back with his dog and let Frances and Michael ride up front. The man, who smelled like pipe tobacco, asked them who Helena was and where they were coming from.

Michael was clever. "She's our governess," he said. "We ran away, and she came to fetch us back, but she's worried she'll be in trouble for letting us get so far."

"Helena is kind," Frances added. "And I'm afraid we were wicked."

This seemed to satisfy the man, and he drove them all the way to Creekmont with no further questions. Helena was able to use a telephone in the general store there, and then they waited for hours and hours, but were told they could have whatever they liked from the shop, including sweets. Helena stopped them just before they made themselves sick.

★　★　★

CHAPTER 37

Travelling by train from Toronto to Halifax, Helena remained their chaperone. Once they'd returned to Toronto, to stay with Helena's extended family there, they were given haircuts and new clothes. Helena was able to contact the Hawksbys in London by telegraph and make travel arrangements. The Children's Overseas Reception Board, no longer active, had no explanation for why Michael and Frances's records had been misplaced. Helena wondered if Theresa and Simon hadn't arranged for that somehow, to keep their secrets safe at Glass Point Lodge.

Frances wanted to walk up and down the train, looking at all the faces and outfits of the passengers, but Michael stayed in his seat. Helena's grandfather had given him a new notebook, and he drew sketches in it without looking at anything else. He hid the drawings whenever Helena tried to peek, but Frances saw some of them. They were of the people and the things they'd seen in the woods around Glass Point—things that looked so ghastly to her now, she could scarcely stand to look at them. She asked him to tear them up. Michael said he did, but she wasn't sure she believed him.

After they ate lunch and returned to their seats, Helena motioned to them to come closer and whispered, making sure no one was close enough to hear, "We need to talk about what you'll tell your new family. They will have many questions."

"What shall we say?" Frances asked. "I don't like to lie."

"But you must this time. Because if you tell the truth, everyone will only think it a lie. You will tell them *some* true things. You'll tell them that you never saw their letters. You were billeted in a place with no telephone or electricity. A very isolated place, where you were bored and lonely. This much at least is true, yes?"

Michael was more than happy to lie about where they'd been. He didn't want to share his memories of their time at the lodge. They were special to him, because he knew he'd seen things no other boys and girls had seen. Sometimes he even resented that he had to share those experiences with Frances. He hoped she'd be able to keep quiet about it. She thought she was quite mature sometimes, but she was bad at secrets.

"But what about our studies?" Frances said. "We're so behind in our reading, and maths . . . We haven't been at school."

"You're both very clever. I have no doubt that you'll catch up before you know it."

The Guest Children

A man walked past in military uniform, and Helena went quiet as she watched him. Once he was gone, Michael looked out the window and saw some great body of water sliding past the train windows. After a while, he heard Helena whispering to Frances.

"What *do* you remember?"

Frances screwed up her face. "I don't like to think about it, so I'm not going to speak of it. I think we should just forget it ever happened."

Michael said nothing, hoping Helena would drop the subject. But she gently took his chin in her cool hand and turned his face to look at her.

"And what about you, Michael?"

"Nothing," he said. "I don't remember anything."

"That's good. I'm glad to hear that."

"And you, Mrs. Heitmann," Frances asked. "Will you forget as well?"

Helena's face twitched a little and she looked away from them for a while.

"How long will you travel with us?" Michael asked, hoping they would be free of Helena soon. "Will you go back home?"

"Not for long. I want to see what is left, and who is left, and if there's anything, or anyone, I need to bring back with me."

She closed her eyes not long after that and fell asleep. Frances did too, her head resting on Helena's shoulder. Michael looked out the window at the forests looming over the railroad tracks. He would miss the trees here, miss the feeling of being so far away from people, so far away from the lights and noise. He didn't like the idea of living in a city again.

When he closed his eyes, he saw his mum and dad, and when he woke, the skin on his face was stiff. He wondered how long it would be until he forgot their faces. At least on Blank Lake, he'd never have forgotten.

They said goodbye in Halifax, where another chaperone had been arranged for the voyage. Helena hugged Michael first and patted him on the head. He frowned and looked at the ground but said thank you and goodbye. When she got her hug, Frances returned it warmly and asked if she could write letters to Helena. Helena promised to write back.

"What do you think will become of Mr. Sturgess?" Frances asked her.

"I don't know," Helena said. "I hope he won't stay there for long."

After their final goodbyes, Michael watched Helena disappear into the crowd. He knew they would never see her again. Just as they would never see Aunt Theresa and Uncle Simon again, or any of the people they'd met in Canada. It would be a story they told sometimes, a story filled with omissions and embellishments, but when it was repeated often enough, it would eventually feel like the truth.

★　★　★

CHAPTER 38

The voyage home was far less exciting, but such is the nature of return journeys. On the third night, Frances woke in the darkness and found their cabin empty. Unsettled, she tried the lights, but they didn't work. She left the cabin and went out into the hall. The ship was pitch-dark throughout, and there was no one to be found anywhere. Frances knocked on doors and ran around the ship, increasingly frantic. Finally, she went up above deck.

It was as dark outside as it was in the ship. She went and looked for the crew, but the whole deck was empty too. Finally, she looked over the side.

The ship wasn't moving. They were no longer on the sea at all. Instead of water, the ship was perched on an ocean of sand. The sand stretched all the way to the horizon, flats and dunes in every direction. All she could hear was that empty seashell sound, the one she'd begun to think of as the sound of her own mind. Refusing to accept what she saw, Frances screamed at the sand, and screamed away the silence.

When she woke, sweating and sick, she saw Michael staring at her.

"Bad dream."

"Yes."

"About what?"

"I felt like I was still there."

Michael smiled and ruffled her hair. "Don't be silly, Fran. It's already a thousand miles away. We're going back to England, and everything is going to be lovely again."

Frances didn't like Michael calling her Fran. He'd never done that before. She decided she needed to get some air, and some certainty that what she'd seen was really and truly a dream. Leaving the cabin, she went up to the deck.

Indeed, there were lights on and people moving about, mostly crewmen who gave her funny looks in her night-dress but decided not to say anything about it. Frances looked across the darkened sea. She remembered seeing the ship sink that night, amidst the convoy of so many others, the fire in the water after the U-boats struck. It was a night she thought she'd never forget, even while she hoped to forget everything that came after.

Frances thought about all the dead men and dead ships whose bones must line the bottom of the ocean after all those years of war. She thought about Stanley too, still floating out there somewhere. The real Stanley, not the false one they'd seen stalking the woods around Blank

Lake. Perhaps some little boy or girl would find him on shore someday. She hoped not.

Frances said a little prayer for the dead, and then decided that she'd be better about saying prayers from then on. After, she stared at the sea, the gentle motion of it soothing her until she thought she might be able to sleep again. There was no firelight from burning ships on this voyage, just a sliver of moon and the little lake of light around the ship, a reverse shadow moving at pace with it through the night sea.

Chapter 39

When Frances and Michael disembarked, they met their aunt and uncle. Alan Hawksby, their father's younger brother, was a kind man. A lawyer by trade, he had a handsome house in west London that he shared with his wife, Eleanor. They had no children of their own, and perhaps for that reason they didn't speak down to Michael and Frances, instead treating them as something closer to curious house guests from a foreign land, whose customs they couldn't quite fathom.

Certainly, their comportment had suffered from their time in the wilds of Canada. More than once, Michael noticed Eleanor watching their table manners with open-mouthed dismay. Eleanor patiently reminded them of proper etiquette, and there were new clothes, books, and even some toys purchased for them. Michael requested a teddy bear, and although they thought he was far too old for such things, they got him one who looked a little like Stanley.

THE GUEST CHILDREN 293

They were to resume their schooling and would need tutoring to catch up on their studies. Alan would frequently tut-tut about the dismal relatives in Canada who'd allowed them to slide so far in their schoolwork and their manners. He often asked questions about Theresa and Simon, but Frances answered in monosyllables, and Michael not at all.

On three occasions, Michael vanished from their house for days, causing a great panic. Each time, they found him in one of the big city parks, hidden away from the world in a small shelter he'd built from rubbish and scraps of wood. Alan and Eleanor whispered in the night, worrying about what to do with this troubled boy who'd become their son.

One weekend, they went and stayed in the family's house by the sea. After supper the first night, they all went down to the beach. They bought some sweets and went for a stroll. Frances saw a couple arguing in their swimming costumes and went into a fit of giggles until Eleanor shushed her. When Alan saw some other children playing on the beach, he encouraged Frances to take Michael over to meet them. Michael was reluctant, but Frances took his hand and strolled over to find three younger boys and two girls building a castle in the sand.

The boys sneered at them, but the girls invited them to join. Their castles were elaborate, with stone ramparts and bits of driftwood and seaweed built in. Frances leapt into action, taking up a mound of wet sand and forming it into something like a grand cathedral.

Michael didn't understand why his sister had become so fixated upon churches and God of late. It bothered him. Any time he mentioned the lodge, Frances would leave the room or simply open her bible and ignore him. Any time he mentioned their parents, she'd grow distant and quiet, and he could tell she was drawing away from him, going to some place where she didn't have to remember painful things anymore.

The girls on the beach were local. They asked Frances where she'd come from. She told them about their voyage to Canada, inventing funny stories about their time there during the war. She did quite a good job of it, and Michael knew that soon they'd both adopt these stories. They'd talk about what was better there, and what was worse. About the tall trees, about seeing mounted policemen in their red serge uniforms, and about spotting a great big bear in the forest.

That lie, like all the best lies, had a little bit of truth to it.

The boys asked Michael why he wasn't building a castle too, but he didn't bother to answer. He wandered off down the beach and kept wandering, even as it started to grow dark.

After a while, he heard Alan and Eleanor and some other adults calling for him in the distance. He wasn't ready to go back just yet. In the twilight hue, Michael looked across the sea. The waves rolled as he inhaled the sour salt of it. The scent brought him back to seaside trips with his parents from years before. He still thought of them every

THE GUEST CHILDREN 295

day, even as Frances seemed willing to let Alan and Eleanor take over their roles without any fuss.

The voices calling his name from down the beach were getting louder and closer, but Michael didn't move. He watched the sea and waited. He hoped that if he waited long enough, his parents would come back the way they had at Glass Point Lodge. It didn't matter where he was, they would find him.

When he found an old dead fish washed up on the shore, Michael buried it in the sand and built a little house on top of it. When it was done, he just sat there, waiting and wishing.

Michael closed his eyes, convinced that when he opened them, he would see his mum and dad standing before him. Instead, he felt a hand on his shoulder. Someone wiped his face. And then he was hoisted up into strong arms and carried along the beach.

So long as Michael didn't open his eyes, he could believe it was anyone carrying him. That it was anyone putting him down in bed, taking his temperature, or squeezing his hand and asking him questions. He kept his eyes shut so long that Alan and Eleanor called a doctor to examine him. The doctor sighed over Michael's silence and his stiff-limbed refusal to be examined. After an eternity, the man gave up and left.

When Michael finally opened his eyes again, he saw Frances. She was sitting on the floor at the foot of his bed, holding his new bear in her arms.

His sister put her finger to her lips, and he nodded, and they agreed to sit there in silence for a while before they went back to rejoin the world. Michael felt that Frances understood him then, and she wanted him to know that. He was glad for his sister in that moment, and almost told her that he loved her. When Eleanor saw Michael emerge from the room, she put a hand to her mouth, then rushed over and pulled him into her arms.

In the weeks that followed, Michael sometimes thought about running away again. He'd go back to the beach to check on the palace he'd made, to see if his mum and dad had returned. At first, he was kept too busy with school and chores. Then, over time, he thought about it less often, until one day he didn't think about it at all. If he ever felt sad about his parents, he just looked at a photograph of them, and usually that was enough.

★   ★   ★

ACKNOWLEDGEMENTS

Many thanks to my editor Holly Ingraham, Thaisheemarie Fantauzzi Pérez, and everyone at Crooked Lane Books for all their help getting this novel out into the world; to Samantha Haywood, Megan Phillip, and Eva Oakes at Transatlantic for all their diligence and support; to Naben Ruthnum for his encouragement to take this on; to the National Archives, the BBC, the Toronto Public Library's Historical Newspaper Archive, and the City of Toronto Archives for their vital research resources; to Janice Zwerbny and HarperCollins Canada; to Devon Halliday, Andrew Pyper, Dustin Alpern, and Graeme Stewart; and most of all to Elisabeth Brückmann, Owen Tarr, Susan Tarr Timmins, Bruce Tarr, and my extended family for always being there for me.